Dedicated to my Granddaughter

HOW TO CUT UP A CHICKEN

DIANE BLOCK

MINDSTIR MEDIA

Published by Mindstir Media, LLC
45 Lafayette Rd | Suite 181| North Hampton, NH 03862 | USA
1.800.767.0531 | www.mindstirmedia.com

Printed in the United States of America
ISBN-13: 979-8-9856345-0-1

CHAPTER

ONE

I can smell the damp soil beneath my cheek. I'm cold, and I hurt all over, but the first thing I sense upon waking is the smell of the earth … the strong breath of life, dark, damp, and full of vitality. Something I don't have much of anymore. The grass I'm lying on is cold and wet. I make a feeble attempt to reposition, but jabbing pain screams out from my left side and my left arm seems to be trapped in a piercing grip beneath my body. I don't remember what happened but I must have slipped on the wet grass and fallen. I probably broke something in my left arm.

I don't know how long I have been here. I don't know if my injuries are bad. They feel bad. I can feel the warm liquid running down the back of my neck, cooling as it slips down. Besides my arm, I must have hit my head. I have a ferocious headache. You never know what kind of weather you are going to get in September in Wisconsin, it is pretty cold for mid September. I knew I had to start cleaning up for fall and winter, especially the bird bath (now the flowing bird feeder). I came out to the back yard to clear branches and weeds, and start cleaning up the bird feeders and bird bath. So many birds have been coming lately. So many crows. All hungry! All wanting more and more.

I don't know for sure what time it is … still daylight though … but I must have missed their feeding. They sound angry, especially the crows. The flowing bird feeder sounds like it is clogged again. Damn! Probably another knuckle stuck in the plumbing.

—1—

Liddie had been born and raised (her early years) on a farm in Wisconsin. She learned early to love nature, and spent many carefree days with her two dogs roaming the countryside of the farm. She didn't really have many chores, so there had been a lot of free time to play and roam around the hills. There were neighbors, but not close, so there were not many other children her age, and those that were, did have farm chores and not much free time. So Liddie spent her days with the two dogs and her wild imagination.

It was an ideal childhood though. Especially the summer days. She would get up early and head for the hills out back of the farm house. From the rocky top of one of the hills you could look out over the farms and countryside. She could stay up on that hill all day. A fresh water spring ran through the property at the bottom of the hill. An apple orchard sat back further on the hill. Wild strawberries could be found here and there, and blackcaps grew down the side of the hill. Liddie would hike about the hill and surrounding areas all day long. As the day started to come to a close, her mother would call out the back door of the farm house and that would be Liddie's cue to come home.

While she played throughout the day, Liddie liked to imagine herself as a good cowboy, rescuing the good and curtailing the evil. Yeah, she knew she was a girl, but she would always imagine herself a "cowboy". Details could get worked out later. She would hold on to this choice a long time, much to the dismay of her older siblings who tried to drive home the realization being a "cowboy" was going to be out of the question.

During the school year Liddie didn't get to be up on her hills as much as she liked, but she still had the opportunity to spend time with her dogs and explore. She had always felt a kinship with nature. You don't have to pretend to be someone you are not with nature. Everyone is accepted, just the way you are. A sweet peace comes when you are not needing to be someone acceptable to others. People are always expecting you to act a certain way, fit in, be what they think a person should be. It can be exhausting to be around people too much. School was okay, but only okay because it provided books and a chance to getaway through those books.

The family sold off the farm when Liddie was going into her freshman year of high school. They moved to a small town not too far away from the old farm, but there were no hills to climb … none that were owned by her family. She did take walks, but this would be in town and people were everywhere. She could never experience the freedom to be just herself while people were around. Those same experiences came with adulthood. She adapted to the constant pressure of acceptance by peers and the social norm of the community. She managed to get through her jobs and raise children without too much difficulty. We all have to learn how to adapt to our circumstances. But "adapting" is not the same as the freedom, and she yearned for the chance to be just herself again.

So, after she retired, and her husband passed, she moved out to a home that her son had purchased. He lived in another state, but purchased the property to retire there himself one day. For now Liddie lived alone, in a nice home, a few miles out from the small town, down a gravel road. There were only a couple houses down this road, and most of those were vacation homes, unoccupied most of the year.

The home was really at a lovely spot. The front yard bordered on the gravel road. The back yard dipped down to the Wisconsin River. There was a small level area in the back for sitting outside (if the mosquitoes didn't carry you off). The back deck looked out over the river from the main floor of the home. Liddie could enjoy the sights and sounds of nature again, though maybe she couldn't trek through that nature as carefree as she had in childhood.

THREE

Today was a lovely spring day. Spring has always been Liddie's favorite season. Things come alive again in the spring. There is always a new hope. Liddie was sitting in the back yard on a bench her children had put back there for her. Snow White, a life sized, ceramic figurine was sitting on one end of the bench, bending over, like she was feeding birds, but there was room on the other side for anyone who wanted to sit outside, Liddie to be exact.

The back yard rolls down to the Wisconsin River (a small inlet). A great place for watching birds and other wildlife further out on the river and on the nearby small islands of the river. The shades of green on the bushes and trees were just beginning to show off their beauty. The ducks and geese were still out on the water. Even the noisy Sand Hill Crane were still there. There was a slight nip in the air today, but warm enough to sit outside. The river water was still cold but already there had been a lot of boaters out. Liddie's house sat far enough away from the main river that she didn't really notice the tourists on the river.

Liddie had a dream to put bird feeders, bird houses, and baths in the back yard, as far down to the river as the DNR would allow. Recently she had focused on a Disney theme. So far she had the Snow White with the bench, and also a Cinderella with her blonde hair pinned up for the ball and the blue flowing hoop skirt. Cinderella was a bird bath with water coming up out of the top of the skirt, and flowing down into pockets all around the skirt, only to be collected at the base and returned again to the top. Liddie had only to keep the hose in the base of the skirt and turn on the faucet every few days, when the water seemed to be getting low.

The back yard did have a bit of a descent, which made it a little difficult for a 73 year old, but Liddie only went as far as the bench most days. The other bird feeders needed to be refilled about every other day, but these she kept closer to the house, away from the downgrade to the river.

Sometimes, especially in the spring, the river would get a little high. Snow melting up north always made the river go up a little but it wasn't too high yet, not over the rocks. No danger of flooding the back yard. The rocks were put in when her son purchased the house, per DNR regulations. It was very hard to walk across those large rocks. Liddie, knowing she was unsteady on her feet, did not attempt to navigate over those rocks. For her, the river was for looking at, not wading in.

Liddie didn't hear the car pull into her driveway. But then the driveway was all the way around at the front of the house. Now she could hear and see her granddaughter, Hannah, and her friend, Sidney walking around to the back. Hannah and her friend were both 17 (going on 30), and, like every teenager ever, knew everything there was to know, as opposed to a 73 year old, out-of-touch, grandmother. But, oh, she loved that girl. Liddie would agree with whatever her granddaughter said … most of the time. Both girls were beautiful girls. Full of life and dreams and no fear of anything this day would throw at them.

"Hi, Grandma." Hannah calls out as she comes around the steps to the back yard. (GMA is usually what Hannah called her).

"Sidney and I were thinking about taking the kayaks out for a little ride up the river. Do you think we could borrow them this afternoon? We will be careful."

The kayaks belonged to Hannah's uncle (Liddie's son), and they didn't normally get loaned out. Sometimes Hannah would take the kayak out with her son when he was home, but Hannah had never gone alone or with another friend. And that water was cold. Right away Liddie was nervous, and it was probably evident in her voice.

"The river is pretty high and it is bound to be cold and rough," Liddie replied. Now Liddie has never really cared much for Sidney. Kind of a user as far as Liddie is concerned. But she is Hannah's closest friend and Hannah is Liddie's only granddaughter … the light of her life. And, Liddie doesn't begrudge much from Hannah.

"We are not children," Sidney complained, with a slight annoyance in her voice. Sidney has never had much of a sense of respect for anyone … elders or betters.

"I just want you to be careful and aware of the dangers," Liddie replied.

"We will be careful, Grandma." Hannah answered. "Are the kayaks in the garage?"

"Yes, and you can use them but please be careful, both for your safety and see that the kayaks don't get damaged. You uncle would not be pleased. Take the life jackets too, please."

It is not easy getting two full sized kayaks down to the river's edge, over the rocks, with paddles and life jackets, but these two young ladies were up for the challenge and soon had the kayaks in the water, were seated, and off down the inlet to the main river, with a lot of giggling and chattering.

Liddie went back to work picking up the yard … clearing twigs and small branches into one pile for her son to burn later in the year. She then sat down for a little bit, next to Snow White, and may have dozed for a short time.

Late afternoon brought two tired teenagers back up the inlet, paddling slowly, and not quite as excited as when they had left. Liddie could see from a distance that Sidney's kayak had been damaged. And this caused distress to Liddie. How was she going to replace or repair that kayak before her son came home? She was on a fixed income. She knew Sidney or her parents would never offer to pay for repairs. Likely Liddie's daughter, (Hannah's mother), would help, or even Hannah, but Liddie did not want to trouble them.

So, Liddie was noticeably upset by the time the girls got to land again, and, evidently, Sidney had been planning her response as well.

Testy and ready for an argument, Sidney began, "It was an accident, OKAY! The current swept me into a big log in the water."

Sidney started with other excuses, her voice getting louder and more abrasive as she talked. Words flew back and forth between Sidney and Liddie. Hannah tried to be the peacemaker but wasn't getting far with this. By the time Liddie was calming down enough to listen, Sidney had stormed off to the car, leaving Hannah to pull up both kayaks. Liddie tried to help but was probably more in the way than a help. Hannah tried to smooth things over and offered to help with repairs, but grandma would not accept her financial assistance. Hannah went to the car then and drove Sidney and herself back to their homes. Liddie just stood there watching the car leave and wondering how in the world she was going to fix this. At least they were alive. The kayaks could have tipped into that cold water. Count your blessing.

CHAPTER
FOUR

"Who was that, Liddie?" Her neighbor called from the porch next door.

Liddie lived off the main road but she did have one neighbor, Claire. They had lived next to each other for a number of years now … sometimes great friends, sometimes complaining foes. They were both about the same age, set in their own ways, and not great with compromise, but it seemed to work for both. Liddle hated when Claire felt the need to mow her lawn at the ungodly hour of 8:30 a.m. (Liddie was not a morning person), and Claire thought the bird feeders were encouraging way too much wildlife to come into the yards (her yard as well, though Claire had no feeders).

They did help each other out from time to time, giving one or the other a ride into town if needed, helping with the snow blowing, though Claire insisted upon blowing snow in the early morning and Liddie knew that stuff wasn't going anywhere till after 10:00 a.m. Sometimes they would sit on one or the other's deck and look out over the river. Claire did not enjoy the quiet scenery quite as much as Liddie did. And Claire thought there might be some sinister reason why Liddie chose to live on a back road like this one. "What was she hiding from?" Liddie would explain again and again that her son had purchased the home to retire away from the city, and she only enjoyed the quiet here. There was no other reason to purchase a home so far away from town or other people.

Claire, by her own admission, did not easily integrate into society. She said she used to have a part time job in town but wasn't able to get along with co-workers or the public who shopped at the little store. She did have a few people who would stop by to visit sometimes; and she mentioned a daughter, but never elaborated on the daughter much. Really it was just Claire and Liddie on this gravel road. They each had their daily routines and preferences on how life should be lived. They tolerated each other, and even enjoyed some moments. It seemed to be working for both of them.

"Just my granddaughter and her friend." Liddie responded to Claire's question.

"Is there a problem," Claire asked, always the nosey neighbor.

"None that you need to worry about. Now go inside and tend to your own business." Liddie fussed.

"Okay, fine. Take care of it yourself then." And with that Claire did go inside, but just a moment later popped her head back out.

"I made some cookies this morning. Want to come over for a cup of coffee and cookies in a bit? You can help me with the jig saw puzzle I am working on."

And just like that, they were good buddies again.

"I will be over shortly. I love those warm cookies." And Liddie also went inside to freshen up a bit before the cookies and coffee.

FIVE

Spring warms into summer. Winter seems to take forever, but the warm, beautiful summer days go by so fast. Liddie had spent many a nice afternoon, and sometimes into the evening, sitting with Snow White. She went out every day to check on the bird feeders and make sure they were full. For tiny birds, those little bellies never seemed to get enough. Mostly there were Red Wing Blackbirds and Wood Peckers, and of course there were always squirrel. Liddie could put bird seed or peanuts in the outstretched palm of Cinderella and the squirrel could somehow make their way up that figurine and get the peanuts in Cinderella's hand. That was okay. The squirrel were as much fun to watch as the birds. Sometimes she would see Finch or Oriole, but not often. Whatever came to her feeders were welcome and good company. Sparrows have to eat too.

The summer had been drier than usual and the inlet was shallow, more so than it had been in the spring, but it was still there. Liddie could look through the brush and trees today and see people out on the main waterway. There were not a lot of large boats out, but down this way you would see more kayaks, canoes, and sometimes people floating around on a rubber tube (not a great idea with the Wisconsin River currents, even in the back waters).

Down the road from where Liddie's home sat there was a public access boat ramp. Often tourists or people from the small, nearby town would come with their smaller boats and get into the river from that boat ramp. Sometimes they would get on the river from a resort further up the river, where it widened. Either way, the inlets often had people floating along passing by Liddie and Claires' houses. The inlet made for a quieter, safer traverse of the river. It also allowed for some nice fishing, especially catfish with all the vegetation growing. Liddie enjoyed watching people float past in canoes, kayaks, or even tubing.

Liddie had been outside with the long handled tree limb cutter, trimming some bushes and low hanging tree branches. As she was looking out over the water, she saw a canoe coming closer and closer to her bank. She couldn't make out who was in the canoe at first, but finally the person came into better view. It was Sidney. It appeared that Sidney was going to stop and talk and Liddie made her way down to the rocks, carefully placing her feet where she hoped she would not slip. Sidney pulled up close to where Liddie was standing, and once stopped, she started to rise, holding the side of the canoe, like she was going to stand up in the canoe to talk.

"Well, here I am again, and in my own boat this time. I don't have to worry about any old bats cussing me out for something I can't control."

(Oh, it was going to be that kind of morning, was it?).

"That's right, Sidney, you do not have to worry about messing up any of our kayaks again, because you will never get to use them again. Is that why you came through all these inlets, just to yell at me?" Liddie complained.

"Listen, you old witch, you don't own these waters and I will take my canoe wherever I want, so fuck off!" Sidney was getting visibly upset now, balancing in the canoe and waving her hands as she spoke.

Harsher words followed, neither of them backing down, one feeding off the other. Sidney appeared to make an attempt to come up off the rocks toward Liddie. Forgetting she had the long handled trimmers in her hand, Liddie raised her hands up to protect herself, and the blade swept across the face of Sidney, just barely, but enough to make Sidney pull back, trying to dodge the trimmer blade, and causing her to lose her balance on the rock she had just stepped onto. Sidney was barely touched by the trimmer blade, but when she went down, she hit one of the larger rocks in the wall with the side of her head. Now she lay there motionless.

And in that brief moment, Liddie's life stopped … forever to be changed. How does life change like that? One second you are a simple woman, enjoying the pleasures of nature, living a quiet but fulfilling life … and that quickly you've become a murderer.

Liddie had never done anything outside the law except maybe push the speed limit. Now here she was with a potential deadly weapon in her hand and a young girl lying there on the rock wall. Blood was pouring from where she must have hit her head, flowing from the rock and into the water. Sidney still was not moving, and from what Liddie could tell, she was not breathing either.

In what seemed like hours, though probably only minutes … maybe seconds, Liddie tried to think and figure out what to do next. But she couldn't think. She could barely see. There was a roaring in her head that would not allow her to think or hear. Everything in her world seemed to stop. Everything was a fog. Liddie just stood there, looking down at the girl. She knew she could not leave Sidney there. She could go inside and call for help. But, even now, she still had the trimmer in her hand, and everyone (EVERYONE) would know that she, Liddie, killed her. Everyone would tag her a horrible, vicious murderer. Liddie had watched enough of Forensic Files and crime shows to know that they would label her a merciless, calculating psycho. She would die in prison, away from everyone and everything that she loved. Liddie couldn't think straight right now, but she could see what her future held. She had to do something. But what?

CHAPTER

SIX

God, please let her be alive! Please help me! Oh, God, what have I done? Please, please make her be alive. I keep saying this to myself, in my head. I keep begging God to make it be okay again. If she just is okay I can get her help. I can make things work out again. Why isn't she moving? Please, please, God, you can make her be alive. You can make things right again. I didn't mean to hurt her. I didn't mean for her to fall. Please make her okay again.

The child still was not moving. Blood started to flow down the rock where she must have hit her head. I can't believe this is happening. I would never hurt her. I did not mean to throw my arms up like that. What can I do, what can I do.

Ten minutes ago everything was normal and quiet. Everything was good in the world. What am I going to do now? Let me see if I can lift her. Let me check and see if she is breathing. Maybe I should run up and call someone. I don't see her chest rising and falling. She must be dead. I can't get down to listen for a heartbeat, or I am going to fall too.

I can't think. I don't know what to do. "Help, someone help me!" I am screaming this in my head but I can't hear anything coming out of my mouth. No one is here anyway.

Wait, here comes Claire. Maybe she can help. I can see her coming, but I can't make out what she is saying. She is running and yelling … like a crazy woman. "Claire, Claire, help me!

No, she is screaming at me. She is blaming me. I can hear her now.

"I saw you! I saw what you did!" Claire was running down the back of her yard into Liddie's yard.

Liddie was still standing over the body of Sidney. Sidney was still not moving, just lying there, her body laying across the rocks, and blood continuing to flow into the water below. The canoe floated gently beside the rock wall.

Liddie still had the roaring in her head and could not hear well, but gradually, as Claire came closer, still screaming at her, Liddie turned to see Claire. Claire was frantic but still had her sense about her, a place to which Liddie had not yet returned. Claire continued to scream at Liddie and accuse her, and Liddie, still trying to process what had just transpired with Sidney, now had to deal with Claire. Liddie turned slowly and looked at Claire. Claire stopped just a few feet from her, probably alarmed by the look on Liddie's face. Both ladies just stood and looked at each other for a moment, until Liddie started to come out of her fog.

"It was an accident. I didn't mean to hit her. She fell. She just fell back and hit her head. I didn't mean to hurt her or make her fall." Liddie cried.

"I saw everything. I saw you raise that weapon towards that girl. I saw you hit her. She wouldn't have fallen if you hadn't hit her. You probably killed her. I'm calling the police." Claire turned to head back to her house.

And once again, Liddie had a second to make a decision. If Claire got back to her house and called for help, ambulance or police, Liddie's life was over. No one was going to believe her. No one was going to understand that it was an accident. She was sure Sidney's parents would tell the police all about the argument earlier this spring. Claire was already accusing and had made up her mind that Liddie was responsible for Sidney's fall and (probably) death. Yes, it would be all over for Liddie if Claire got to that phone. And even if Liddie could convince Claire right now that it was an accident, and not to call anyone, how long before Claire would change her mind and call anyway. No, she could not let Claire make that phone call.

And in that quick second, Liddie raised that tree trimmer one more time, letting it fall hard against the back of Claire's head. Claire was a couple years older than Liddie, and no match for the full force of the tree trimmer. Claire went down hard, face first, on the branches and grass of Liddie's back yard. Claire, like Sidney, did not move. But now Liddie made a conscious decision to finish the job. Claire could not get back up again. Liddie had made too many bad decisions in just a few moments. The quiet, passive life of this grandmother was now turned upside down and she would have to do whatever she needed to do. She needed to make sure Claire was dead. The trimmer came down again and again. This time from a cold, calculating killer.

CHAPTER

EIGHT

have to stop her! I have to stop her! Claire is going to ruin everything. She isn't even going to give me a chance to explain. Don't you run away from me! Don't you get back in that house and call the police! My thoughts have gone from compassion for the girl to abject fear for myself. I have to stop this descent into madness right now. Claire needs to be stopped. If she would just listen to me for a minute, but she won't. I know her, she will just run with her own mind set on what she thinks happened. My God, Claire, stop!

She isn't turning around. She won't let me talk to her. I have to take matters into my own hands now. "Claire, Claire, why did you make me do this?" Claire is just lying there now. I couldn't let her get back up ever again. Once I dropped the clippers I had to make sure it was over. "I'm so sorry, Claire. You made me do it." How many times did I hit her, I can't remember? I just knew I needed to stop her from getting back to her house and calling the police.

Now ... now what have I done? How could I have done this? Never, never did I ever think I could do something like this.

I have to sit down. I have to get my bearings.

"God, why did this happen?" I can't think, I can't move. I wish I could die right now. "Just let me die too, God. There is no reason to live anymore. My own life is over too." What am I going to do now?

CHAPTER
NINE

After the blows ended, Liddie fell down in a heap on the grass. The reality of the last 15 minutes began to set in for her. The weight of what she had done felt like a huge weight across her shoulders, not allowing her to move or stand. How evil could one person be? How could she ever have done something this horrific? She could barely kill a bug. How does a person go from living the quiet, unassuming life that she had, to taking a life, no two lives, and even though the first was a mistake, the second, for sure, was a deliberate act. Oh what a tangled web we weave…! There was no going back now. She must do whatever she must do.

Liddie looked around at her back yard. She realized the first thing she would need to do was get rid of the bodies. Sidney would be easy. Place her body in the canoe and take it out to the open waters. Let the Wisconsin River currents take care of the rest. Surely it would only be a matter of time before someone would be looking for her.

Now, it is not easy for an older woman to get across the rock wall, find her footing in the water, and lift a young girl's body into a canoe. This was something she never thought she would be able to do. But she had never been this scared before, and maybe there was something to this adrenaline thing.

First, though, Liddie had to hide Claire's body. Claire and Liddie lived pretty much alone here, but there were houses further down the gravel road and who knew when someone might drive by. Drivers wouldn't be able to see the body from the road, but there was no sense in taking chances. Liddie had been trimming branches much of the morning, so she took those cut off branches and laid them over Claire's body. If you were looking for something, or just walking around in the back yard, you could certainly see the body, but Liddie was hoping no one would be walking around in the back yard until she could do more to cover up the body.

Right now, she had to clean up the bloody rock wall and get that canoe and body down to the open, swift main part of the river. This would not be easy. The inlet would float a kayak or canoe, in most parts, down to the main portion of the river; but there were areas you had to pull it over sand or branches that had fallen into the water. In some areas it just wasn't deep enough to get through easily. Liddie had on only casual shoes. They were already filled with water and did not provide a dependable foothold. Each step was dificult and had potential for a fall, and Liddie did fall a few times, but desperation is a great motivator. Liddie would take a step and pull on the canoe, take another step and another pull. And so on, falls and all, she made her way down to the opening of the river.

She hoped there would be no one on the river. She had no protection from witnesses because the branches that had hidden her as she made her way down the inlet, were gone. She took a good look up and down the river and across to make sure no one was watching her. Her vision wasn't the best but today she would just have to hope no one was watching and get the deed done as quickly as possible. She waded out to the deep as far as she could go without getting caught in the current and tipped the canoe enough to let Sydney's body fall from the canoe. Then she allowed the canoe to fill with water and sink. Good decision or not, it was done, and she made her way back to take care of the next body.

Claire was not going to be so easy to dispose of. Liddie really did not know what to do. She was pretty sure no one would be looking for Claire for a while. Claire had children, but they didn't visit often. Liddie didn't know how often the children would call. But surely Liddie would have a few hours, maybe a day or so, to figure out what to do with the body. She was pretty sure she couldn't just dig a grave. There would be investigations when they did discover Claire was missing. Cadaver dogs, physical evidence. Liddie had watched plenty of crime shows and knew some of what they would be looking for in evidence.

Liddie decided to drag the body to the entrance of the basement. It was hidden from view, both from the river area and either side of the yard. There was a drain there and Liddie put the still bleeding body over the drain, maybe making it easier to clean up evidence. Liddie wished she had paid more attention to those crime shows, but who knew she was ever going to need that kind of knowledge. Never had she expected her life would take this turn.

When she finally got Claire's body where she wanted it, over the drain, next to the basement's sliding glass doors, Liddie sat down on a couple sand bags that had been left there from spring. Finally, the reality of the situation engulfed her. She could not have stood up if someone was forcing her to do so. She sat on those sand bags and sobbed, shaking uncontrollably. They had to be silent sobs, Liddie didn't want to alarm anyone who might possibly be in the area, but they were soul crushing sobs.

Liddie could see no good way out of this. There was no explanation she could give anyone. The fatal blow had been to the back of Claire's head, when her back was turned to Liddie. Liddie couldn't claim some kind of self-defense. Any investigation would figure out what the weapon had been, and that it was a murder. Liddie sat there until way past dark, staring at Claire's body and trying to think. Trying to figure out the best course of action to take. She may have even slept fitfully that night, on those sand bags.

In the early dawn, Liddie went out to the shed and got a tarp to cover the body until she decided what to do next. A plan was forming, but carrying it out was not something she was sure she could do. There was no way Liddie could get that body out to the little islands along the inlet of the river. She could possibly bury the body out there if she could pull the body out, but Liddie didn't think she could do that even with the help of the tarp for dragging. The "super Liddie" strength she had with Sydney was long gone. She could barely stand by herself now. So what must be done? She would have to take the body out in pieces.

When she was a child her mother had raised chickens, and every fall they would butcher and can the chickens they raised in order to have meat on hand for the winter months. Liddie had cut up her share of chickens. Can't be that different, can it?

CHAPTER
TEN

I have no thoughts. I have no feelings. I am crying, no sobbing. The kind of sobbing that makes you hiccup, not allowing you to catch a breath. I am shaking so hard. I don't think I can do this. But I can't just leave things as they are either. I have to do something. For what seems like forever I stand here looking at the body. I have lost who I am. I have no values, no strength to do the right thing. I have no guidance and structure to make the good decision, because I am no longer that person. I have never learned how to be the other person, the person full of rage and evil, one that could easily do what I'm about to do. Yet, I must do something. My God, what kind of monster have I turned into?

CHAPTER
ELEVEN

I t was early morning, around 5:00 a.m. maybe. Liddie didn't check the clock, she just knew the sun was starting to rise. She went upstairs to the kitchen and got the biggest and best knife she could find. Her son had a chain saw in the shed but Liddie didn't know the first thing about handling a chain saw. That would have made too much noise anyway, and Liddie didn't want to make any noise, no alerts to anyone. This was the day after since the girl and Claire had died, and Claire's body would have to be taken care of today and tonight.

The situation had been very traumatic up until now, but this next step would be more than even her fear and desperation could handle. Liddie thought of the prospect ahead of her, knowing what she was about to do, and she began crying and shaking again. One bad decision, made in the blink of an eye, brought her to this. One bad decision upon another bad decision, and now she was likely making another bad decision. But would any step, after that first swing of her arms, have made any difference in the outcome? Probably not. Her only hope now was to continue and try to hide everything from those who could put her away for the rest of her life. And that would be short, as Liddie knew she could never make it through the process itself, let alone years in prison.

Just like cutting up a chicken. Just think of it as cutting up a chicken with Mom. When she first started it was with one very large kitchen knife. It didn't take long for her to realize that was not going to be effective. Liddie went out to the shed to see if there might be a good saw or better knife. What she found was a short handled hatchet ... looked a little like a small ax. That would have to do.

When you cut up a whole chicken, you pull the thigh away from the body in the opposite direction until the joint displaces. Then you cut away the tendons from the dislocated joint. The same with taking off a leg from the thigh. The same with a wing. This eliminates the need to cut through a bone. When all the extremities are removed, you bend the lower torso backwards, bending the spine, and when it dislocates, you cut at that spot where it is just nerves and tendon again. The most difficult is cutting the breast portion in half. You need to cut down hard through, or on either side, of the breast bone, bend each section back in the opposite direction, and then cutting where it connects and snaps on the back. Fairly easy on a chicken.

Liddie started with the head. Of course, when you are dealing with chicken, the head and the feet are the first to go. The chicken is still alive when the head comes off, but one quick chop takes care of the head.

Liddie knew she had to get the head first. The thought of Claire looking back up at her filled her with horror. The only way she was going to get through this was thinking "chicken". A gray head of hair and bulging eyes was going to negate any thought of "chicken". The feet and the hands also had to be cut off. Nails (both fingernails and toe nails do not decompose easily and provide DNA. These would have to be taken out whole, with the head, and buried. This being the first job, also became the most traumatic and most difficult job of the whole process. It had to be done.

Taking time to calm herself, Liddie then began with the hip and the leg … pulling the joint in the opposite bend until you hear the crack of the joint, then cutting against that joint until it is severed. A human hip is a lot more difficult than a chicken thigh/body connection, and it took a while to severe the hip from the body, but eventually she got it. The same technique with the arms. The head severed, with feet and hands, the body cleaned out, and everything into doubled up black garbage bags—sobbing the entire time and stopping only to catch her breath and get her balance enough not to fall over, (If she fell, she would likely pass out herself and she needed to get this job done), Liddie continued with the terrible task of dismemberment.

Now she just had the torso. And working this the same as a chicken, Liddie made a couple cuts of the skin/muscle on each side and bent the torso back until she heard the crack of the spine in the small of the back, then she began cutting where the crack had displaced from the spine. The upper torso, same as a chicken, would have been to cut down the breast bone up, but this was not working with a human. Try as she might, she could not dislodge the upper torso. Something would have to be done, as she knew she could not pull or carry that entire upper torso, even in a garbage bag. Using the hatchet, Liddie came down hard, two, maybe three times across the breastbone area. It took a long time and great effort, but she finally succeeded. The upper torso was in manageable pieces.

Liddie was exhausted by this time. It was late afternoon by now. No sleep, the exhaustion of the entire day before, the mental fatigue, the emotional mess … it was all overwhelming.

She made her first attempt to take the smallest of the bags out to the islands that dotted this portion of the river. She had a small shovel that she took with her, but she still couldn't handle the shovel and even the smallest of the bags. How was she ever going to get the biggest of the bags out to the islands?

It was then that Liddie remembered after cutting up the chicken, her mother had put the chicken, bones and all, into jars and then pressure cooked it for safe keeping for winter. It was worth a try. Liddie had plenty of Mason jars with lids available. She had often pressure cooked fish, the kind that had too many bones (Carp, Suckers, Cat Fish), so that you didn't have to deal with the bones so much. Pressure cooking made the bones softer and chalky almost, and easier to digest if you happened to ingest a smaller bone. It was worth a try. This time, however, Liddie would pressure cook everything, as much as she could get in her pressure cooker safely, before placing it in the jars and sealing again with the pressure cooker. This would mean stripping all the bones of everything that could be cooked in the pressure cooker.

And again, Liddie began to cut up. And again, the tears flowed and the shaking started, but oddly, it was easier this time. She had gotten through the worst of it and she was still alive and not yet exposed. Maybe things were not great, but they seemed to be getting better, and maybe there might be a promise for the future.

All night, again, Liddie, canned raw meat, including all organs. She even included small bones. She had cleaned the bigger bones as well as possible to make it lighter and easier to carry out to the islands. As everything began to cook down, she would take out the resulting "broth" (an exaggeration but it did look like a broth of sorts), and place it in a large bowl, well, many large bowls, as many as she could find, and then let the pressure cooker cool and rest a bit. She didn't need any problems with the pressure cooker at this point.

Finally, by early morning, everything had been cooked down and placed in bowls, all over the kitchen. Now it was time to put into Mason jars and pressure cook again. And Liddie had to get the left over bones and head out to the islands before it got dark again. She knew she would never get back from the islands on her own after dark. Liddie filled the Mason jars, as many as she had (she would have to run into town tomorrow for more), and started the pressure cooker again.

Liddie had a little while to get the first set of bags out to the islands once the pressure cooker was set. It would turn off on its own once the timer was set. Liddie knew she would continue to fill jars and cook all night, but now … now it was time to dig.

CHAPTER

TWELVE

There are no words to express what I am feeling or thinking. I stand here with my kitchen knife in my hand and wonder what the hell I am doing. This is not even human. I cannot even blame a monster for what I am about to do. Monsters don't do this kind of thing. Even wild animals do not do this. They kill to eat. Crime shows would be pressed to come up with an adequate description of the person who does something like this.

My God, what has become of me? Is there another way out of the mess I have created? I can't think of one if there is. Maybe I should just call the police myself right now.

I try not to think at all. Just do the thing I need to do. I try to concentrate on chickens. I try to remember my childhood and canning with my mother. I will just allow my mind to go blank. There is no saving this situation or myself. I will just complete what the plan is in my head. I have thought about it and this is all I can see now. Tomorrow will have to justify itself. I will face my demons later.

— 25 —

I t was a trek to get out to the little islands that popped up when the river ran lower. For someone who was afraid to even get too far down toward the river's edge before this, it was a big step. But then, there had been so many "firsts" in the last 76 hours, and this would not stop Liddie. She made it down the yard, across the inlet and to the second in a series of islands with shovel and bag in tow.

It had been treacherous, falling down so many times, trying to get past roots that lay just below the water, getting stuck in the muddy ground and then laying down everything to retrieve her shoes out of the muck. She eventually found ground that was dry enough and above the river enough that she could possibly dig. She found a spot, a little bit away from the water (so it wouldn't unearth her secret too soon), and began digging. She made it fairly deep, though probably not the usual six foot, maybe 3 feet, except for the bag with the head, hands, and feet. To bury these she would have to dig an extra deep grave. Hair and nails do not decompose easily and she didn't want a casual kayaker to come across a floating head of gray hair any time soon. Yes, she was sure she would be caught but hoped it would not be right away.

Then it was a trek back, check the pressure cooker, and put a new batch in, and get the next bag. She did leave the shovel at the site so she didn't have to carry that also. Back and forth, check pressure cooker, new batch, back to island. Another day gone. Actually, it was well past nightfall when the last bag (with head, hands, and feet) made it to the island. At home, with everything put away in jars, stacked in the basement for now, Liddie cleaned the entrance to the basement, where the dismemberment had taken place, and then cleaned and burned her clothing that she had been in for the last three and half days/nights.

Then, and only then, could she lie down to rest. Even as tired as she was, sleep did not come for some time. Every time she closed her eyes, there were visions of all the horrible things she had done. She was sure that she was scarred for the rest of this life, and probably the next.

Sleep finally did come. She woke the next morning to a knock on the door. One of Claire's daughters had called for a wellness check on her mother. A man, middle aged, well dressed, was standing at her door. He did not ask to come in. (Thankfully as the kitchen really had not been cleaned last night). But he did ask if Liddie knew the lady next door and if she had seen her in the last couple days.

Now Liddie had never been a good liar, but she had never been a killer before either and it seems she had winged that pretty well. So Liddie explained that she had not been feeling good the last few days, and though she did know the lady next door, she, herself, had not been out and about, so, no, she had not noticed anything different. The gentleman thanked her for talking to him and asked if he could stop back another time, maybe when Liddie was feeling better.

Liddie told him, "That would be fine, I want to help in any way that I can." She asked about Claire's welfare, as any good neighbor would, but the gentleman was not forthcoming and said his goodbyes. And with that, he left. And Liddie went back to sleep again. No bad dreams this time, no worries, no guilt … not anymore.

LIDDIE

I am so tired. There is nothing left in me to cry out. My body continues to shake uncontrollably but it is only from exhaustion now, not because of the mental anguish of what I am doing. I will deal with that later. I have made so many trips back and forth from house to the island … dragging heavy bags, digging, burying, and back to the house. Physical exhaustion is blocking out the horror of my actions. That is a good thing, but I know it is waiting for me to deal with later.

I need to rest. But can I sleep? My life is upside down. I don't even know who I am anymore. I lie here and try to close my eyes for sleep, and all I can see if blood and bones and flesh. The mirror of my actions come flashing back at me. I should have died myself. I should have let Claire live and died myself.

Thoughts, fear, anguish, sorrow … deep, deep sorrow …

FIFTEEN

Liddie slept most of the rest of that day, rising only to use the bathroom, and then sleeping again. There were dreams and demons, but mostly she just slept. When she woke, early evening, she decided to clean the kitchen. There were still bowls sitting around and these she placed in the refrigerator. They would need to be poured into Mason jars and pressure cooked again. Tomorrow she would go into town and get more jars.

After cleaning the kitchen, thoroughly, Liddie went down to the basement again and cleaned the entrance again (using bleach). After the cleaning, Liddie went to the yard and got handfuls of dirt to attempt to splash the dirt around where the area had been cleaned. She threw a few dried leaves and branches over the area as well, hoping it would look natural and untouched. Liddie knew from her shows that an investigator would notice if that area looked too clean.

Liddie surveyed the jars she had placed on the one wall of the basement last night. What was she going to do with the contents of those jars? She really could not just leave them there. She would think on it. She did have a lot of raccoons that came into the yard at night. They would eat anything. Maybe she would put a bowl of the "broth" out tonight and see what might happen.

Sure enough, the bowl she left outside in the back yard that night, was completely empty the next morning. Possibly tipped over, but there didn't appear to be any evidence of small bones or flesh left around the area. Only a cadaver dog would know if there had been something here. There was always a chance cadaver dogs would be brought in, that she knew, but if there were no tangible evidence at all, and Liddie would make sure all tiny bones or flesh were gone, they may not place a lot of importance on the dog's acknowledgment of a cadaver being there.

The following days were nothing out of the ordinary. Liddie had gone in to town to get more jars, these had been filled and cooked in the pressure cooker again, and were now on the shelves in the basement. Every night she put out a bowl for the raccoons, until Liddie was down to just what she had canned. She noticed the crows and even a few ravens had been coming around during the day and they were looking in the area where she had left the bowls for the raccoons. That gave Liddie an idea.

The next day, before she turned on the faucet to refill the Cinderella fountain, Liddie emptied two or three jars into the base of the fountain. She stood back and watched what might happen, and just like the water, this mixture started flowing up to the top of the skirt and down into the pockets on the skirt, then down to the bottom and pulling back up to the waist to flow down again. She sat down and watched from her perch on the bench to see if the birds would notice the food was coming out into the pockets.

It did take a couple days, but soon the birds were flocking around Cinderella like crazy. They seemed to enjoy this new bird food. More and more birds came flying in each day. And they seemed to know when she was filling it again. They would chatter in the tress, presumably spreading the news, that it was dinner time. Liddie enjoyed watching them all come in. She liked listening to the chatter and liked to pretend that she could talk to them and they could understand her, just as she thought she could understand them. These were her new friends. This was a beautiful new world for Liddie. She planned to keep her new friends happy and content for as long as she could. She had quite a few jars still on the shelves, but these birds were going through it fast. Maybe she could find some commercial bird feed that these birds would enjoy just as much. She had time to search and see what she could find, and she would find something they really liked.

CHAPTER
SIXTEEN

My life is calming down. It has been a crazy few days. I have worked like I never worked before, more than any day in my younger years. My body hurts, but not as bad as my heart and soul hurt. Whatever I have coming in this life or the next, I deserve it. I do not understand why God allows me to continue living. I would rather be dead and face my judgment now. But I don't die. I continue on and carry this burden of horror in my soul. I have covered my trail of blood-shed from human eyes so far, but not from God's eye. I can't cover what troubles my soul.

Yet, each day comes and goes a little brighter than the last. I am sorry for my friend, Claire. I'm sad and so sorry that I snuffed her life out so quickly, but she had every intention of ending mine in a very different way. If only she had been willing to hear me out and talk things over with me. I know she was upset and I know I shouldn't have raised my hand to Sidney, but it was an accident after all. Claire could have at least listened to me before running back to turn me in to authorities. She didn't even consider me. I'm sorry about Claire, I really am, but I'm glad I am alive and still have my life here.

I may only have a limited time before someone discovers what I have done, but I will take whatever days or months I have. And I will enjoy them. Right now I have to look at the present and not let the past stress me. There will be a time coming for stress. I will enjoy my birds, my space here by the river, my peace … if only for today.

CHAPTER

SEVENTEEN

The rest of July and the beginning of August went by peacefully. The body of Sidney and the sunken canoe had been found. There wasn't much of an investigation. There was a gash on the back of Sidney's head, but it was presumed that was a result of her falling out of the canoe and hitting her head on a rock or some sharp branch. There was no autopsy done, per the family request, and the acceptance of death by concussion and drowning prevailed. That being a plus for Liddie because, with an autospy they probably would have discovered Sidney was dead before she hit the water. That could have meant a long and potentially damaging investigation, damaging for Liddie anyway.

Investigators continued to visit Claire's home and inspect the area around her house. There was an investigator, a Mr. Benson, who would visit with Liddie a couple of times. Liddie talked with him and they would walk together in the back yard and discuss Claire and her habits, her possible friends, or if Liddie thought she (Claire) would take off on her own—those kinds of conversations.

Liddie was quite calm and forthright with her answers to the investigator. Liddie told him she didn't think Claire would go off on her own, but she might have taken a little walk down by the river. There was a sandy beach down the inlet where you could sit with your feet in the water. Sometimes Liddie, herself, would walk down that way.

Actually Investigator Benson and Liddie became quite friendly with each other. Investigator Benson treated Liddie like a favorite auntie, and Liddie actually enjoyed conversing with him. Life had gotten quite lonely now that she had no one to argue with (Claire) or visit with. Sometimes they would just sit in the back yard and he would look out over the river and islands and the vegetation, and you knew he was trying to think of what could possibly have happened to Claire.

But a body was never found, no evidence to suspect any foul play at the house. (The door had been unlocked and a little ajar when Claire disappeared). No signs of burglary, nothing destroyed or knocked over in the house. The car was still in the garage. It was all very puzzling to the poor investigator.

A cadaver dog had been brought in, but only went along the river that bordered Claire's house and out towards the main river, out toward the sandy area that Liddie had told the investigator about. Evidently they thought maybe she had drowned. They never brought the dog over to Liddie's property. Liddie didn't know if the dog would have been able to pick up a scent from the month or so before, but it never been a problem.

Things were actually working out very well. Liddie started to think maybe her life would be okay after all. Maybe no one would ever know. Maybe she would be able to live her life without repercussions for her deeds—at least in this life, but she knew the next life would be different, there would be a balance due. For now, the days were going well.

She did spend a lot of time feeding the birds. Mostly crow and ravens now, and once she even saw a large, old vulture out near Cinderella. That was a little scary. That vulture kept coming back too, once it realized the food was to its liking and was replenished every day.

Occasionally there would be a very small bone or fleshy substance that would get caught in the plumbing and cause the flow to come to a stop. You knew there was something stuck by the way the plumbing would gurgle and grind, never coming to a halt, but like a straining motor. Liddie quickly learned how to clean this out and get things going again. Once there was what looked like a knuckle and it was very difficult to get this pulled out of the plumbing, but she finally got it. Thankfully, because when the flow stopped, the crows started complaining again. Crows can be very noisy, very demanding!

And Liddie's social life (limited though it was) got back to normal as well. She went into town to shop, she would stop at the library for books, or visit with some of the clerks at stores she frequented.

Once in a while she would meet with her daughter and granddaughter. They might go to the state park that was near. They might meet for lunch. There was never any indication that things were different or unusual in Liddie's life.

On occasion they would come out to sit on the deck and watch the birds below. Family seemed a little distressed by the type of birds that frequented Liddie's feeders but Liddie was not concerned and eventually they stopped expressing concerns. Liddie's daughter and granddaughter had busy lives, and they didn't come out often. Her son planned to return home for a visit the last week of September. Liddie kept in touch with everyone mostly through social media.

Liddie's days were filled with routine. A routine that she had come to enjoy. Mornings were always hectic. Most people would be concerned about the variety and number of birds hanging around Liddie's back yard, but by afternoon the crows and vultures (many now) had moved out. After the yard was free from these larger birds, the song birds came in for the sun flower seeds and suet Liddie still put out. The afternoons in the back yard were very pleasant. Evenings Liddie would retire into the house, with windows open to listen to the night sounds, until she went to her bedroom. The raccoons still came around but Liddie did not have much to give them, but they never stopped searching.

The line of Mason jars on the shelf were depleting rather quickly. Liddie was having a hard time keeping up with the appetites of the birds. They were pretty insistent if she fell behind filling the feeders, especially the Cinderella feeder. She was getting up well before 8:00 a.m. now, much to her dismay. If she slept in, she could hear those birds just carrying on something terrible.

Once they were fed, all was well, and Liddie could spend the rest of the day sitting and watching all the wildlife: birds, squirrel, even an old beaver came up from the river inlet. He kept his distance, but he would peak around the trees at her and she even gave him a name, Charlie. She loved seeing new animals and birds every day.

And it stayed very pleasant right up until the day Liddie poured the last of the Mason jars into the Cinderella fountain. That day went well. The next day began noisy as usual in the morning, but by the third day, and the fountain was just plain water again, things started to get testy.

CHAPTER
EIGHTEEN

I miss my family and going into town. I have missed Claire so much, much more than I would have ever thought. I used to think we argued all the time, but she really was a good neighbor and friend to me. It is lonely out here without Claire.

Investigator Benson stops by now and then and we sit in the back yard and talk. He is such a sweet young man. I feel badly sometimes realizing that I am withholding from him, but only sometimes. My life has a renewed joy now. My birds are happy, I have peace—even though I need to keep some things blocked off even from my own thoughts—and I have my freedom. I have everything that would have been taken from me with the first loss of life. I am reasonably happy. At least for now. I will worry about the hereafter another day.

I am a little worried though. The jars are almost gone and I don't know what I am going to feed the ravens and crows. They seemed to have enjoyed this new meal. I hope I can find something.

CHAPTER
NINETEEN

The fourth day, after the jars were completely gone, Liddie awoke to the usual complaining of the crows, ravens, and now a pretty good number of vultures. There was nothing to give them but the usual suet, sun flower seeds, and variety of song bird food she had available. She had searched. She purchased bags of mealworms. She even hunted night crawlers by flashlight at night. They did not want that. Some of the birds had developed a new taste, and they wanted what they wanted. They did not go away that afternoon. They sat in the trees and made a horrible commotion throughout the day and very early the next day.

Towards the end of that afternoon, four days without their usual fare, Liddie went out to the mailbox to get the mail. The crows followed her. Crows are very smart. They can recognize a person's face. They know when they like a person and when they don't, and they convey that dislike to other crows. These crows may have liked Liddie at one time, but that was wearing thin. They wanted their food. One even took a dive at her as she came back to the house. Thoughts of leaving the house at all began to frighten her. She stopped going out for the mail, allowing it to pile up. She let the garbage pile up too, missing the usual pick up days. Going out to the car was completely out of the question. The birds would attack for sure, and she feared falling while she was running. Missing the mail was fine, there was never much in the mail anyway, but groceries were getting low and Liddie knew she could not get to the car fast enough to avoid getting dive bombed. And how would she ever get back in the house negotiating groceries. This was becoming a problem. She needed to think of something … something to appease her new bird population.

The aggressive birds started to hang out on the upper deck, looking in at her through the main floor sliding glass doors. They would sit on the railing of the outside deck and watch her. Every morning there seemed to be more crow and raven, even an occasional vulture, sitting on the deck and deck railing. Sometimes the vultures would peck at the sliding glass doors, and she didn't know how long the glass would hold up. Liddie had become trapped in her own home.

Her daughter and granddaughter would ask how she was doing (phone or message), and ask about coming out, but Liddie would make an excuse to not have visitors. She did not want them discovering that there was a slight bird problem. Too many questions would come up and there simply was not a good, acceptable explanation. Liddie feared she would not be able to put them off much longer. They just might show up anytime.

TWENTY

Many years ago, when she was much younger and stronger (physically and emotionally), Liddie had wanted to make some kind of difference in this world. She wanted to make a difference in someone's life … help them along, as she had been helped and encouraged by so many in her life. She, and her husband at the time, had taken into their home someone who was down on their luck and needed a helping hand. Sometimes that resulted in a big change for the person who needed help. Sometimes, not always, it was the quiet moment they needed to get back on their feet and move on in their life. Liddie and her husband enjoyed the feeling of believing that they had, in some small way, provided encouragement to another person. After all, we all need each other. We all need a helping hand at some point in our lives.

Sometimes this opportunity would be all they needed to get started againg, be successful, and their success was wonderful to watch. However, sometimes all the giving and helping would only result in a slap in the face. People are different. Some are grateful for help and you remain friends for years. You watch their lives change and that person grow. But for some, you can do everything, you can give till you have nothing left to give, and they want more, and they are angry when you can't give more. It takes its toll on the giver.

Cal, it turned out, was of the latter sort. As a matter of fact, the experience Liddie and her husband had with Cal, had caused both to realize they could not continue to do this sort of thing anymore. It was just too taxing. Cal was one who just could not change his behavior. When things were going well, and he was getting everything he wanted, Cal was a very happy young man. When times were tough, not only for Cal but also for Liddie and her husband, Cal wanted to go back to the easy cash life. Fuck Liddie and her husband, and all their house rules.

When Cal had been living with Liddie and her husband he (they) had been going through a tough time, little cash flow, little available for their own necessities, let alone all the "needs" that Cal thought he had to have. The family had been through this before and it just took a little patience and a little luck, and a lot of work, for things to get better again. Cal was never very good at waiting. He wanted instant gratification.

Cal, still living with Liddie and her husband, began dealing again. A whole new group of people began visiting at the home, all hours of the day and night, waking the family, disrupting family activities. These were not the kind of people Liddie, or her husband generally invited into the house. They were not accepting Cal's new "friends". Liddie would come home from work to find the same type of people hanging out in the living room. She would go for a drive with her husband and come home to friends sitting outside with Cal.

They talked to Cal and asked him to either get his own place or meet his new friends elsewhere. Cal didn't want to leave his good situation just yet. Finally, Liddie decided to try some tough love when Cal rebelled against the situation and the thought that he might actually have to work or leave. She told Cal he could do what he wanted on his own, but, if he were living in their house, and they found out he was going back to his old ways, she would be the first to turn him in to authorities. Cal's response, "Snitches end up in ditches. And sometimes their families." That was the last straw for Lidde and her husband and she would never forget that threat. The threat to her and her husband did not mean much, but no one—NO ONE—threatens the family.

Liddie drove Cal and his few things down to a cousin's home in Milwaukee. He planned to live there until he got his footing and found his own place, either in Milwaukee or Racine. He hadn't decided yet. He was not happy when he had to move from the home and life he had become accustomed to, but it was time for him to be on his own. Cal knew this too.

Liddie had not heard from Cal since that day. She had heard about him from others. It seemed that things were not always going well for him, but he had not called or messaged, or even written … until very recently.

About June, Cal had found Liddie on social media and they had messaged back and forth a little. Liddie was thinking about Cal while she sat in her home, plenty of time on her hands, trying to figure out what to do about the birds.

Aileen Wuornos, before she died, said something along the line of: after the first couple killings, it gets easier. That is probably very true, because Liddie now just needed a meal for her angry birds. And she knew the best way to get it, and who to invite to dinner.

TWENTY ONE

LIDDIE

'm sitting here thinking about all the young men who came to live with us, years ago, when I had enough energy to deal with it all. (Certainly not anymore). The good times and the bad times. And there were good times. I have had the privilege of meeting some remarkable young men. Some going through hard times, some just being young. I certainly did not make very good choices every day when I was young. Sometimes we just need someone to have our back while we go through those years.

It is so good to still have contact with so many, mostly through social media, but sometimes I get a phone call. Even more rare, but so nice, I get a visit. And it is such a joy to see their families and see how they have met life's challenges and come through, though not always unscathed … we never come through life's challenges without scars, none of us. But most are doing good, very good.

Most of them are a real joy. Not all. Some have even lost their lives already because they just could not change. One very nice young man, so intelligent, so respectful, could not overcome his addiction to alcohol. He once said, "One drink was never enough, and more than one was too much." He had died trying to rob a liquor store years ago. Another had been found in a river, a drug deal gone bad. Some just could not get their life on track. Some were a joy, some a challenge.

Cal was a challenge, but he had found me on social media recently and we had been messaging. Cal and I had enjoyed messaging (well, I enjoyed his messages. I can't say if he enjoyed mine.). He seemed to be doing pretty good. I'm glad for him. But I have never forgotten the time he threatened me and my family. I think it is time to invite him to dinner.

TWENTY TWO

Cal, who was always looking for something free, eagerly accepted the invitation to dinner, but might need a little money for gas to get there. Liddie sent him enough for gas and started planning his meal. She knew what he liked, she had fed him often enough. She was sure his appetite had not changed that much over the years, though it had been a few years since she had last seen him.

Cal liked his drink, one of his weaknesses, his taste for alcohol. Liddie didn't usually have alcohol around the house, but she searched through her son's stash and found something Cal might like. During the late night hours she ran into town and shopped. The crows had been awakened when she went out, but didn't chase after her.

The next night, just as Liddie had requested, Cal drove in the driveway after dark, and parked his truck around the corner by the edge of the garage, just as Liddie had requested. He walked over to the door, where Liddie was waiting and gave her a big hug.

"Oh, it was going to be 'Happy Cal' tonight!" She thought to herself. "Well, maybe for a while."

They sat around the table enjoying a light meal. Liddie was not really sure how her plan might be affected by the food she was serving, but she didn't want to make the meal to heavy, nothing to reduce the effects she was hoping for from this evening. Following the meal, Liddie made a nice, big drink for Cal. A drink that would help him relax. She pulled from her knowledge of crime shows again, and had added one more ingredient to this drink, a big helping of antifreeze. If the amount she gave him didn't kill him outright, maybe it would slow him down enough to get him downstairs tonight. She knew she could finish off the rest. The two sat and talked for a while, until she saw that he was becoming a little lethargic.

Liddie must have done something right. The drink or the antifreeze did slow him down, but still alert enough to make the stairs to the basement. He didn't understand why he was going to the basement but he followed her downstairs, with a little help. Liddie just kept telling him she had something really cool to show him. In his altered mental state he complied easily.

Once in the basement, Liddie opened the sliding glass doors and led him out to the entrance. That very busy entrance from weeks earlier. One quick chop with the same small hatchet she had used before, brought Cal down to the very spot she needed him, directly over the drain. He didn't even realize anything hit him. He went down so easily. And the rest went just as it had a few months earlier … the cutting, the packing of cleaned bones, the pressure cooker, the canning, the cleaning.

This time there was no rush to move the bones. First the birds needed to have food flowing through Cinderella before the dawn. And that is just what Liddie did. The very first batch didn't even go into jars. By early light, before the birds were even making noise, Liddie took the water hose out of Cinderella and poured from a bowl the "broth" remains of Cal.

After the first batch flowed through as it should, Liddie started the trek again out to another of the small islands. Only one bag this morning. She would take the rest out later. She no longer feared going out to the islands after dark. She had learned to put her fears in perspective, and the birds were far more frightening than a walk through the inlet and the islands. She had made this trip a few times and knew the way pretty well. No chance of getting lost.

This last killing did not phase Liddie a bit. As a matter of fact, she almost felt justified. No one threatens her family. Besides, if he wasn't planning on using her, he never would have made the trip for dinner. He probably thought he had found another resource again, the old bitch was rich again.

Liddie went about her day the next day, without a care in the world. For that matter, there was nothing to fear. No one knew, she supposed, that Cal had planned to visit her. No one could trace him to her. Well, with the exception of the truck in her driveway, beside the garage. But she would be able to get rid of that soon. It would mean a little bike ride after she dumped the truck, but she could do it. And Liddie could enjoy the next few weeks with contented birds again.

— 45 —

TWENTY THREE

LIDDIE

I t was a long bike ride back from the lake where I left the truck, somewhat submerged in the water. I couldn't take it all the way in the water (to hide the truck completely), because I was afraid I would not be able to get out safely from the driver's seat. I tried to wipe off anything that would imply that I was in the truck. I don't know if I got it all. I did get the bike from the back before it went in too far. I know they will find the truck and find out who it belonged to.

Hell, for all I know, he stole it from someone.

But it was a long bike ride back home. I had to get off and lie down in the grass as soon as I saw car lights, behind or ahead. I didn't want anyone to see a little old lady riding a bike in the wee hours of the morning. Questions, questions! I didn't need that.

Yes, I know I will get caught sooner or later. There is going to be a time when they figure out this little old lady is not the sweet thing she puts on. I know it will all end eventually. I will have to pay my dues. But, for now, I am good. For now I can take care of my birds. For now, I am going to get some rest. I have not ridden my bike so far, for so long, in a very long time. I am exhausted. Feed the birds and go to bed.

TWENTY FOUR

Once again the birds were happy, which meant Liddie was happy. She had spent a couple sleepless nights again, cooking, canning, cleaning, and toting large garbage bags, but all that was over and she could return to her life that she enjoyed. How little it takes to scorch the conscious ... and her soul was scorched. She was able to shop, get her mail, sit outside in the back yard again, have company over ... and she did.

Investigator Benson stopped by one last time to check on her. His investigation had been placed in the cold case file for now, and he just wanted to see how she was doing. She sat in the back yard with him for a while and he admired the Cinderella and Snow White. Of course, he had seen them many times before but then it was an official visit and they really didn't have time to talk about her bird haven. He did remark that she needed to have her water quality checked as it didn't look very pure. She said she would certainly get that taken care of.

And life went on. She told herself she had gotten away with three crimes. Three! A misplaced pride welled up within her, and a confidence that she would now continue on peacefully until she could figure out how to deal with the birds. Three was enough. She didn't want to use that means again. Luck could only carry you so far. Liddie did think about what she should do. How she should deal with the birds. They still were there every morning, waiting for her to bring the food they expected. The jars were emptying out pretty fast again. Liddie still had not come up with a plan. What would she do? How to get rid of these awful birds ... these hungry birds? Maybe get a pellet gun? Maybe try to scare them away? But she didn't think crows scared very easily.

Liddie was out working in the yard again one day in mid September. A beautiful day for September, but then most days in September are beautiful. She had a renewed confidence in her ability to walk around the back yard. She had trekked up and down, over the rocks, in and out of the water, shoot, she no longer feared walking around in the back. Pride goes before a fall, in this case, literally. She had just filled one of the song bird feeders when her ankle turned or she slipped on something, she didn't know really what it was, but she felt herself going down.

CHAPTER

TWENTY FIVE

’m lying here, drifting in and out of consciousness. I can hear the birds around me cawing and flying about. I can see one vulture, there may more, but lots of crow and ravens. Meat eaters all of them.

I can hear the Cinderella sputtering, like something is stuck in the plumbing again. I try to move, but the pain is just too great. I lose consciousness again. Again I wake and the fountain is still sputtering. I cannot fix it and the birds are not getting their food flow. They are hovering ever closer to me. I feel a pain in my leg and look down. The vulture has taken a big piece of flesh out of the calf of my leg. It hurts, but I shake my leg to make him fly away and the movement hurts so much I lose consciousness again. I don't think he has moved far because I wake to pain in my back. Another piece of flesh gone.

It is cold lying here, and there is pain in my left arm, but also from my head. I must have hit my head on something when I went down. My phone went flying when I fell and I can't reach it now. No one is around to hear me calling. Claire would have helped if she were here.

I feel another smaller peck, but still painful, and this time it is one of the crows. I swear, I recognize its face, much like he/she probably recognizes my face. And the crow looks angry. (How do I know what an angry crow looks like?). Another piercing pain, this time in my thigh. Another vulture.

Is this to be my penance while still here on this earth? Probably. And what will I have in the next life. I am so afraid after all the horrible things

— 49 —

I have done. It is so hard to stay conscious now. I drift in and out, always waking with a fear that I am no longer in this world and my judgment lies before me. But each time I wake again it is because of a peck … vulture or raven … and it reminds me that I am still in this world. I am in pain and miserable but I am not ready to face the judgment I will have to face.

And now they are all coming. It is breakfast for the birds. I wonder if anyone will find me before there are only bones to bury? I will not be here much longer. It is time to pay the piper.

CHAPTER

TWENTY SIX

Investigator Benson had to make one more visit out to Liddie's home. The family had called asking for someone to do a wellness check. They had not heard from her in a couple days, and they feared what they might find. Investigator Benson offered to make the run out. The family drove out but waited for the police before going into the house. Benson knocked on the door but when no one answered, he went down the yard to where they always sat and talked. There he found Liddie, or what was left, lying by the bench. The birds were still feeding though it looked like they had feasted well. The flesh that still remained closer to the underbody. The eyes were gone, much of the scalp, and the arms and legs were almost picked clean.

Benson quickly went back up to the family before they wandered down and guided them back to their cars, hoping he could have the body removed and that he would be able to talk with the family before they saw the carnage.

After calling in assistance, removing the body to a local funeral home, and helping the family back to their cars, Benson walked back down the hill. The birds were still hovering and he could hear them in the trees, but they were not flying about. He sat down for a moment and tried to figure things out. Evidently she had fallen, but why the vicious attack of the birds. Vultures will take the opportunity for a free meal, but there had been a lot of crows here for a residence.

As he sat and thought, he heard the sound of the Cinderella fountain gurgling and straining. First he unplugged the fountain from the basement entrance outlet, then walked over to the fountain, setting his hand on the skirt to steady himself as he checked it out.

"Oh God!" He yelled, as he pulled his hand back in disgust. What is that? The substance on his hand and on the skirt of the Cinderella, felt sticky and smelled terrible.

"What in the world?!" He would need to have someone come in and test this. "What could be causing this bird bath to be so nasty?!"

BRIDE
DOLL

CHAPTER

ONE

"I'm just lying here in bed listening to the kids talk in the living room. They can stay up so much later than I can. But I still enjoy listening to them talk and laugh. Sometimes it gets quiet out there, when they don't agree on something. Then one or the other will start up a new topic of conversation and the talking and giggling begins again." Peggy thought to herself, as she lay in her bed, just a little down the hall from the living room.

She has two totally different children, three years apart in age, but they might as well be from completely different parents. They are so different in personalities and beliefs. Her daughter, Kathy, and her son, Jeff, had not been close growing up. They are growing closer as adults, but still miles apart in life philosophies.

"I should be thankful." She thought now. "At least one is not pushing the other down the steps or chasing the other around the house with a baseball bat. They have matured a little bit over the years. Tomorrow my son will go back to California. My daughter will go back to her husband tonight. I am going to miss them both."

Kathy was a traveling nurse and she and her husband, Wyatt, would head out for the new assignment tomorrow morning. For Peggy, by tomorrow afternoon, it would only be the sound of her own voice.

"Talking to myself (which, yes, I do a lot), or the meows and purrs of my cat, Ginger, will be the only interactions when they both leave. Tomorrow I will be alone", Peggy thought to herself.

Peggy rolled over and thought about how she always gets so very sad when Jeff would leave for his California home. He owns this home in

Wisconsin and comes back often, but always there is that empty, alone feeling when he leaves. When he is in Wisconsin she has purpose again. She is a mother. A roll she has learned how to do pretty good over the years. Even after 30 years of the children being grown and on their own, she can't seem to find another roll to fit into. Nothing works as well as being a mother, but now it is a "mother" no one really needs. Even their father has gone. He is in a better place and he doesn't even need her anymore.

Slowly she drifted off to sleep to the sound of their voices in the living room. She woke briefly when she heard them saying good night in the hall just outside her bedroom.

The next morning was an early wake up as Jeff had to catch an early flight. He packed up his things and they walked out to the car together. Jeff knew his mother always hated to see him leave, but he still had to get back to his wife and home and work. Jeff and Tess didn't have any children, but they have a couple of very spoiled cats. Jeff had followed another girl out to California but always intended to come back to Wisconsin to live. Tess had always lived in California and it was going to take some talking to get her to Wisconsin, especially in the winter. So far, that did not seem a possibility. But he still had a good job out there and couldn't risk letting that job go to move back to Wisconsin yet. So it would be a few more of these quick trips back to Wisconsin to work on projects and visit Mom. He hated to leave her feeling sad but she always got through it and back into her routine after a few days. All would be well.

Jeff and his mother talked on the way to the airport. It was only an hour drive and he had everything ready, so when he pulled up by the sidewalk, he had only to jump out and get his things. No sense in prolonging the inevitable. Mom kissed her son goodbye and adjusted the seat to her short legs (Jeff was 6'3"), and drove off waving and gulping back tears. Always tears. There were always tears, though she tried never to let them escape until after he left.

And now the silence. Only thoughts going through her head. Sometimes it was hard to tell if she was actually talking to herself, or if the words were only thoughts in her head. I guess that is how it goes when you are alone too much of the time. The emptiness of the car now, and the house when you get back home, is so overwhelming. Especially when that morning, and for a few days prior there had been lively conversations. How deep and loud the quiet became.

For the rest of this day, Peggy would watch some of her favorite TV shows, or nap in her reclining chair. She had tried various things over the years to ease the sadness when everyone went home. Depending on the time of year, she would take long walks, go for drives, read outside, or maybe go to a movie. But this was winter and Peggy did not drive well anymore in winter. Every darn thing scared her now. So today she would just watch TV and sleep in her chair. We would figure out tomorrow, tomorrow.

CHAPTER
TWO

Peggy slept well that first night alone again. She did wake up a couple times and remembered she was alone in that big house. When Jeff was home she didn't need to worry or be concerned. She shouldn't have to worry anyway. It was a safe neighborhood, and nothing had ever really happened. It is just that knowing there is someone else there to be with you is comforting. Alone is always alone.

The next day things would start to get better. She would get back into her groove again. First thing always was to gather all the dirty laundry, clean the upstairs bathroom and bedroom (as much as possible, as his things were often everywhere), and clean up downstairs, where she spent most of her time. Peggy would spend this day keeping busy with the essentials of clean up. It always helped to keep busy like this. It made her feel like a mom again. That night she woke up and listened for sounds that had become comforting but there were none, no light snoring, no moving about in his bedroom. This night she would be able to go back to sleep without tears though. It was getting better.

The next new day arrived with the sun shining. Peggy did not care for winter anymore, but at least the sun shining gave hope that spring would come again. It was cold out, but the sun shining in through the windows brightened her spirits.

What to do today? Laundry was done and put away, clean up complete. It was too cold to go for a walk and there would be no driving on these bad roads. It had been enough of a challenge coming home from the airport the other day.

Maybe look through the hope chest and relive a few memories. That always filled the heart. Peggy cleared off the top of her cedar chest and started looking through. So many things in there that brought back sweet thoughts. Kathy had already been given many of the special items that belonged to her childhood. Kathy had her own cedar chest. Peggy had given Kathy about half the love letters Peggy and their father had written back and forth over the year he was in Vietnam. There were other things but Peggy couldn't remember what now.

Still the cedar chest held quite a few things that would be just Jeff's one day. There were the other half of the love letters. And so many little things from Jeff's childhood. The crayon drawings he had made when he was just a little boy. The cowboy boots. How did he ever have feet that small? It was fun just to look over each item and remember.

Peggy had a couple of her dolls from childhood still in her cedar chest. There was one baby doll, made mostly of rubber she thought. And there was another doll made of straw and cloth. A couple of much smaller dolls in fancy saloon dresses. These were very old also but she couldn't remember what they were called.

One by one she picked up things, remembered the year, sometimes the very day, and placed them back in a new corner of the chest. Soon everything had been touched by both hand and heart and put back. And it was still early in the day. Then, Peggy remembered there were other plastic tubs in a corner closet in the basement that held precious memories too. So, down to the basement, with a small sitting stool in hand, she went. Might as well sort through the tubs.

CHAPTER
THREE

Ginger, Peggy's Tortie cat, usually stayed in the house with her, and Ginger had to be in the same room with Peggy. So, Ginger also came down to check out the basement. Ginger had a love for the basement anyway. She would often spend time during the night patrolling the basement. Peggy never knew for what, but often during the night Ginger would set off the Ring system that had a camera in the basement. Peggy didn't even check it anymore when the ring warning went off. Ginger was an older cat, and very, very independent, but needed lots of love on her terms. She appeared to be tough and uncaring, but Peggy knew better. She knew Ginger was a tender soul. It had taken Peggy a long time to win her trust and have her believing that her momma would not hurt her. That little kitty's soul had been wounded and Peggy believed Ginger now felt loved again.

While Ginger was touring about the basement, Peggy moved the furniture that was sitting in front of the closet door. It took a bit because rarely did she ever go into this closet. She had put away tubs of things she didn't want to give up when she first moved into the house after her husband had passed. She wanted to keep these things, but rarely even opened the containers. As a matter of fact most of the containers had come unopened from the last house. Years probably since they had been opened and searched through.

One such container held her Grandmother's quilt that she had made by hand way back in the 50's or maybe 1960's. Dee couldn't remember when. But it was given to her when she married. A beautiful quilt made from scraps of old clothing. Her grandmother had never been anything but poor, but she made blankets out of the smallest scrap available. And Peggy knew those blankets would be warm because they were huge and oh so heavy. Now there were light weight comforters to keep you warm at night. Still, Peggy could not get rid of this blanket made so carefully and with a caring heart. She didn't even take it completely out of the plastic tub, afraid it might fall apart in her hands. Someday, the children would go through these things and this quilt, from a great grandmother they didn't even know, would not have a significant meaning to them. They could get rid of it without feeling too badly. Peggy would leave it in the container for now.

Another container further back held old dishes her mother had given her maybe 40 years ago. They were lovely dishes, but not really useful. Peggy had a bad habit of breaking anything that was remotely breakable, so she carefully lifted them out of the container and as gently, placed them back, before she did let one slip from her fingers. Age did not seem to make things better when it came to dropping and breaking something.

And so on and on through various containers and tubs Peggy passed that day. She was almost to the end of the closet when she spied one more, big plastic container. She had even started putting containers back in another orderly fashion when she saw this one. Alone, and way under the basement steps, it sat. She pulled it out and looked over the contents. There, she found a large stuffed teddy bear. She remembered clearly the day she brought that teddy bear home. Peggy had two older sisters, eight and ten years older. They had all been at the county fair that day. An uncle on their father's side had played a ball toss game and won a teddy bear for both older sisters but ran out of money before he could get one for Peggy. She was only 4 or so at the time and he was sure she would forget. But the younger of her sisters didn't think that was right and had given Peggy that last teddy bear won. There it was. Lying face up. Black and what was once white, one eye missing. It wasn't so much the teddy bear that moved her, but the love of that sister to let her have that last teddy bear won. Peggy had kept that teddy bear all those years. And now here it was again, reminding her of family love.

Peggy was getting ready to put it back and close the lid when she spied what the teddy Bear had been lying on all those years. Her bride doll. Back in the early 1950's bride dolls were a big thing. All little girls wanted to have a bride doll. She surely wanted to have one. It had been a lot of years since she saw that doll. She didn't even realize she had saved it. But here it was. Time to rescue her beloved bride doll from the plastic tub. So, picking her up gently, dress slightly tinged yellow with age, and hair a bit messed, Peggy brought her out from under the teddy Bear and into the light of day. With her childhood prize in hand, she put away the rest of the treasures and came back upstairs. Tomorrow she would figure out a place of prominence for her bride doll.

CHAPTER

FOUR

Peggy had saved a child's rocking chair that her children had used (well, fought over) when they were younger. Now there were no little children left at all. Even her granddaughter and grandson were grown adults. But she kept this little rocker and today she found a nook in the living room, placed the little rocking chair in that corner, and placed the bride doll in the rocking chair. The bride doll was made mostly of wood, the knees didn't bend so the legs went straight out from the seat. If you stood the doll up on her feet, she could walk by raising the arms, alternately, one at a time. Raise the left arm and the right leg would come forward; raise the right arm and the left leg would come out. And that is how a child could "walk" the bride doll down the aisle. This was way cool back in the 1950's. But today, her bride doll just sat in that corner, in the rocker, looking very beautiful and almost royal.

> *A wooden doll. In a white wedding dress, yellowing slightly with age. Painted eyes, pink cheeks, red lips, brunette curls, slightly messed. Painted little black high heels on legs and feet made of wood.*

Ginger did not seemed impressed by this new addition to the living room. She went up to the doll and took a sniff and then backed away hissing. It was probably the smell from being kept so long in that plastic container, and under the teddy bear. Whatever, Ginger would get used to the doll.

Ginger went back to her perch on the back of the sofa. The cat had a favorite blanket that she enjoyed laying on and looking out the sliding glass doors in the living room. Not much to see out there but snow, but Ginger enjoyed looking out from her warm, comfortable perch. Today, she kept a wary eye on the corner where the doll sat.

That night, Peggy woke up to Ginger crying from some distant corner of the house. Wailing was probably a better way to describe the sound. She could hear Ginger, but could not figure out where the cat had gone. Peggy went down to the basement, pretty sure the cries were coming from there. She wanted to locate and help her cat. She searched and called out to Ginger until about 3:00 a.m. but never could locate the cat. She called and tried to soothe Ginger but it just was not working. Peggy finally came upstairs and went back to bed around 5:00 a.m. and slept for a few hours but woke again to Ginger crying. This time Ginger finally came to her when she talked the cat out of her hiding place. Peggy gently picked up the frantic cat and tried to calm the kitty in her arms. The little heart was beating so fast. Poor baby had been so upset and all night too.

Peggy walked the cat back up from the basement but every step up to the main floor found the cat more agitated. Finally, in the living room, Ginger struggled so badly that she tore up Peggy's arms and neck as she tried to get free of the embrace. Ginger was terrified, running from room to room. Peggy didn't know what to do but she needed to let the cat get somewhere that she (the cat) felt was safe. Safe from what, Peggy didn't know. Finally she opened the door to the outside and Ginger went bolting outside. Ginger ran off the deck and into the foot deep snow. Peggy followed. She knew Ginger would not last long in this cold weather and the cat had never been out in the snow for very long. Ginger, however, was not going to be coaxed back to the house or even the deck. For the rest of the day, Peggy attempted to win her cat back to the warmth of the house. When that didn't work, she made a shelter of sorts in the shed that was nearby. Maybe Ginger would go into the shed for warmth and rest. Peggy took food, Ginger's favorite blanket, and lots of straw to make something warm for the cat. All day she coaxed and begged, but Ginger never came back to the sanctuary of the home. She would go into the shed, but not any closer. Peggy was so worried about the cat she had loved and had been her companion for so many years.

CHAPTER

FIVE

"Let her go!" The "voice" came to Peggy out of the blue. And with a sinister tone to it.

"What!" Peggy thought to herself. "Where did that thought come from?"

That was something Peggy never would have thought to herself. But no one else was in the house. And why the malice?

Peggy went into the living room, after all the arrangements for Ginger, and sat down in her reclining chair. Not much sleep last night, and out in the cold all day, she was exhausted. Before falling asleep in her chair, she looked over at the bride doll in the rocking chair.

A wooden doll. In a white wedding dress, yellowing slightly with age. Painted eyes, pink cheeks, red lips, brunette curls, slightly messed. Painted little black high heels on legs and feet made of wood.

As Peggy drifted off to sleep, she thought she heard someone say, "You love that flea carrier more than me. You put me in that tub with that smelly bear."

The voice (probably only a result of a dream like state) had woken her again. She went over to the bear. She started remembering out loud the day the sisters and their uncle had been at that fair. The day her sister had given the teddy bear to her. What a thoughtful, loving gesture. Peggy stroked the teddy bear and she remembered out loud how much it meant to her.

That night, before retiring to her bed, Peggy went out one more time to check on Ginger. The cat, nestled in the blanket but still freezing, wouldn't even get close to her. Tears filled Peggy's eyes. She loved this cat so very much and couldn't figure out what had happened to make her so frightened. Peggy's heart was broken.

As she came back into the house she looked over and saw the teddy bear that had been lying on the sofa, ripped to shreds. The cotton filling coming out of the open rips in the black and white cotton body. Legs ripped almost completely off at the seams. The other eye dangling from his face. Peggy was in shock. There was no one in this house but her. What and why? This little treasure from her childhood destroyed!

Peggy's attention was drawn again to the doll in the rocking chair.

A wooden doll. In a white wedding dress, yellowing slightly with age. Painted eyes, pink cheeks, red lips, brunette curls, slightly messed. Painted little black high heels on legs and feet made of wood.

CHAPTER

SIX

Peggy would sit and study the doll for moments at a time. Finally she got up to fix the messy part of the doll's hair. Peggy remembered when she first got the doll and she had decided to comb out the hair. She was maybe 6 at the time and her mother had stopped her from combing after just a few strokes, because, Mom said, "You will mess up the pretty hair and not be able to get it back to how it looked before."

Mom was right. The part that Peggy had combed, just a bit as a child, never looked quite the same as it had when the doll was new. Peggy really wanted to fix that little bit of hair she had messed up so many years ago.

"Don't touch my hair! You did this to me, don't make it worse!" The voice coming into Peggy's head again. But from where? It couldn't be the doll. Peggy looked deeply into the face of the doll. No movement, no lips working, The lips, eyes, facial features were all painted on wood, but the thought, the words, if you will, were coming from somewhere and it sounded like it was coming from the doll.

"Do you remember the night you had the dream, when you a child?" The doll "spoke" again.

Yes, Peggy had never forgotten the dream. The doll had been sitting in her bedroom, in another child's wooden chair, and the doll had warned Peggy in the dream to never love anything more than her (the doll). It was a frightening dream really. The fear of betraying that doll still lingered in Peggy's mind and heart. But it had only been a dream. Real enough to frighten a child, but surely it was only a child's nightmare.

Peggy spent that night in the reclining chair, afraid to move to her bed, afraid to take her eyes and mind off the doll in the corner. Finally she drifted off into a fitfull sleep.

The next morning she got up to check on her cat and take out some food. She noticed there were no birds at all at the feeders. Usually the birds and squirrel were fussing and fighting each other for the best spot at the feeders, but today, and thinking about it, maybe yesterday as well, there were no signs or sounds of birds or squirrel. Not even a stray cat which often sat somewhere in the yard waiting for a free meal. All was silent.

When she came back inside, she opened the door and tripped over something in her path. She hit the wall of the hallway hard, and, as she went down, and banged the corner just above her left eye. Picking herself up, she looked around for what might have been in her way. She thought she had noticed something, a stick or something poking out from the doorway of the kitchen. But nothing was there now. She looked quickly in the corner where the doll sat.

"Why, on earth, would she need to check the doll," She thought. "It was a doll. Not capable of walking without help. A doll! Not a living thing." But that is where her mind went. Something sinister, something evil, some lingering feeling from her childhood dream still clung to that doll.

A wooden doll. In a white wedding dress, yellowing slightly with age. Painted eyes, pink cheeks, red lips, brunette curls, slightly messed. Painted little black high heels on legs and feet made of wood.

CHAPTER

SEVEN

"Are you happy that you found me?" Bride Doll asked Peggy.

Peggy knew the doll was not really talking, but this has been going on now for a while and Peggy also knew these words were not coming from her own mind.

"I am glad that I found you. And I'm glad that you look as lovely as ever." Peggy said to the doll.

"Except, of course for my hair."

"I can fix that, I think." And Peggy rose to go fix the doll's hair that she messed up so many years ago.

"Don't touch my hair!" The doll screamed.

"I can fix it and then you will feel better."

"How can I ever feel better? You kept me in that tub, under that smelly, disgusting bear, for all of those years. You were supposed to love me better than everything. Did you? NO! You forgot about me. You neglected me. Everything else is in that cedar chest, lovingly taken care of, but not me. NO! You keep me in a tub in the basement for all those years, under a nasty teddy bear." The doll ranted on and on. "I want to sleep in the cedar chest tonight. Put me in the cedar chest."

Peggy, remembered her cat, remembered the teddy bear, remembered the dream; and she didn't want to put the bride doll in the cedar chest. Only bad things could come from that, she was sure.

"Not tonight." Peggy said, quietly. Daring to defy the doll.

"You better be nice to me," Doll said, quietly also, but with an evil tone. "There could just be another fall."

And now she knew. She knew what had made her fall and hit her head. Somehow she had known it all along, hadn't she?

That night, afraid, but realizing she had no other choice, Peggy placed the bride doll in the cedar chest along with the other dolls and all her treasured memories. All night Peggy could hear horrible sounds coming from the cedar chest. She wanted to believe the sounds were of her own imagination but she knew they were not. Peggy was a woman controlled now. No one to help. No one would ever believe her. But she had known somehow that this day would come. She had known ever since that dream as a child.

The next morning Peggy went into the cedar chest to get the bride doll out and place her back in the rocking chair. And, as suspected, everything was destroyed. Every precious treasure, just a memory now. Nothing could be held above or even close to the bride doll. The doll knew when her heart went to something /someone else. Peggy would be the emotional subject to this doll now. She placed the bride doll back in the chair, and closed the lid of the cedar chest. The bride doll knew she had won. She knew.

MEANWHILE

CHAPTER
ONE

Dee clicked on "save" and turned off the computer. She had been writing this story for months now. Or trying to write it. The story was not going quite the way she wanted. It was not coming about quite the way she had planned. Some of the story was true, and getting that part down was easy. She did get the bride doll for Christmas the year she turned 6, or was it 7? She did try to comb the hair and messed it up terribly instead. Around the age of 13, still keeping the doll in her room, she had a dream one night. She awoke to what seemed like the doll looking her straight in the eye from where the doll sat. It was pretty eerie, even for a 13 year old's imagination. In the dream, the doll had warned her never to love anything more than her, the doll. And that dream had stuck with her.

Dee knew that the doll probably was around somewhere. Boxes had been packed up when her own parents had moved into an assisted living and passed out to individual siblings. Dee was sure there were many of her childhood things packed away in the basement closet. Things that she had just moved every time that she moved. But she had never taken the time to look through these various boxes. Maybe one day soon she would search for the doll and see if it still carried that feeling of doom and gloom she remembered.

In the meantime, she struggled with how she wanted that storyline to go. Would "Peggy" end up at the bottom of the basement stairs, as she had considered for an ending. And how would she proceed with the story line after the incident with the cedar chest. She knew there would be more to follow, but she just didn't know what, or how to proceed.

Sometimes the progress of a story is so clear. Sometimes you can actually visualize a story or hear conversation in your head. But recently, this story had become nothing more than a blank piece of paper. Nothing was coming about in Dee's head. She might as well have been searching a blank, white wall for answers. There would be no new additions to this story tonight.

Dee got ready for bed. She was hoping something might come to her mind once she relaxed. It happened that way sometimes. Whole scenes would come into her head. Entire conversations that she would later put into written form. She could hope.

Tonight she slept fitfully. She dreamed of that doll. Actually, she had hated that bride doll. It was stiff and pretty much useless to a small child. You couldn't do much with it other than "walk" it. It didn't open and close its eyes like her rubber doll. You couldn't undress and dress it. She had to stay regal … in her wedding dress. She dare not mess up the pretty dress or take it outside to play. And there had always been something about that doll that made her a little nervous. Of course, she remembered the dream, but there had been more than that threat. It was as if the doll were someone so important that she (the doll) needed special attention and Dee would be the servant. Dee dreamed that the doll was back now, to cause problems.

CHAPTER
TWO

"Click, click, click". Dee woke from her dream with a start. She wondered if the clicking noise she had just heard had been part of her dream (and what had she been dreaming about?), or if it was really a noise that had awakened her. She listened intently, but could not hear anything more. "Must have been just part of something I was dreaming," She thought to herself. She lay down and returned to a better sleep.

The next morning, Dee woke up feeling drained. Those days when you have slept but still feel exhausted. She started doing menial activities about the house, but quickly tired of that.

"What is troubling me," She thought. Something was weighing on her mind, but she couldn't put a finger on it.

She sat down to the computer again and read over what she had already written, but still couldn't find a next chapter for Peggy and the Bride Doll. Maybe it was time to put this one back on the shelf. Maybe coming back to it someday would bring a closure to the story later.

But it wasn't the story that was troubling her. It was the doll. What had happened to the bride doll after the dream, so many years ago? Shortly after that time of her life she had moved into another small town and lived with her sister, taking care of her sister's two children. Her parents had moved from that house and packed up all her things when they moved. They had made sure the things that belonged to each child were packed up and provided for them. Dee was sure the doll must have been somewhere in the tubs. She had not looked through those tubs for years. Right now they were sitting in a closet under her stairs. Maybe it was time to look through her old belongings.

Actually, Dee's mother had never been one to save a lot of things. There were a few things from her childhood, but not a lot. Dee sorted through and made a pile for disposal, and a pile to save and preserve. It was kind of fun to look back on so many things that brought back so many memories. And, yes, she did find the doll. Considerably worse for wear after all these years. The hair was not only messed where she had tried to comb it as a little girl, but it was completely flat from laying under blankets, stuffed animals, etc., all these years. The doll was not even as regal and lovely as she had originally thought. Dee wondered how she could ever have been impressed or frightened by this doll. And how did it stay in the back of her memory all these years, so much so that she had intended to write about it. This doll was nothing more than carved and painted wood, with a couple hinges and rubber bands to make it walk.

Dee placed the doll back in the tub and picked up the materials she had sorted to throw out. Maybe she would sit down and try to finish up that story the best she could. She liked the ending, and maybe she didn't need anything more in that space where she had left off with all the question marks. Maybe she just needed to be done with this story.

CHAPTER
THREE

Sometimes Dee knew it was time to end a story when a new story line or character started to invade her thoughts. But this time, nothing new was coming to mind. Her thoughts were still on that doll. It was confusing. Why was she so obsessed?

She went about cleaning, doing little things just to take her mind off the story and the doll. She sat down in her chair to watch something on TV. Not much was on and it wasn't long before she was napping in her chair, catching up on the restful sleep she had not gotten the night before.

Sleeping so soundly in her chair, as she often did, she woke again to a noise she was not sure was part of her sleep or real.

"Click, click, click"

"Click, click, click"

This time a foreboding feeling accompanied the sound she heard. But this time she was deep enough in her sleep she couldn't wake up right away. She simply knew she did not want whatever was proceeding towards her—and she had a sense it was proceeding towards her—to come too near. No sense of advancing evil, no horrible music, nothing she could see, either in her dream (if it was a dream) or as she slept, but a knowledge that whatever was walking toward her, and she did believe the "click" was a walk, and was foreboding.

Finally she was able to wake from her sleep in the chair. Night had come on. Even though it was winter, and night came early in the winter, she had slept a long time in her chair. Evidently she was much more tired than she had realized.

Dee got up and made herself a light dinner. She watched a few shows on television, and turned in for the night.

That night she slept well, even though she had napped generously that afternoon, she was still tired. Lately it seemed her dreams were more exhausting than being awake.

The next day, after thinking about the items she had went through in the tubs, she decided it was time to do some cleaning and downsizing. She would take the nicer things she had found to a local thrift store. Maybe another child could use them. She had always taken good care of her toys as a child. Now they were still in good shape, for the most part.

Dee went to retrieve those items she had set aside by her staircase, and went through a few more tubs to see if there were more to go to the thrift store. Finally she came again to the bride doll.

"There is no sense in keeping a doll you never really liked." She thought to herself. "Might as well see if another child, or maybe a doll collector will enjoy having this. These bride dolls were quite popular back in the day."

Dee loaded everything up and headed for the thrift store. A St. Vincent de Paul was just down the road. There were places you could put items in bins in the back of the store. She unloaded into different bins and asked for help if she didn't know where everything went. Having accomplished a cleaning up of the closet, she felt quite pleased with herself, and headed home.

Once home Dee felt like she had really accomplished something that day. Maybe she would sit down and see if she could finish Peggy's story. Now, where had she left off...

BACK TO
PEGGY

CHAPTER

EIGHT

Peggy sat down in her chair, watching for any movement, anything in the eyes of the doll, expecting to see her maybe come to life, but there was nothing. There was no movement, no eye contact. How could there be?

This doll was made almost entirely of wood. It was not something possessed.

> *A wooden doll. In a white wedding dress, yellowing slightly with age. Painted eyes, pink cheeks, red lips, brunette curls, slightly messed. Painted little black high heels on legs and feet made of wood.*

Peggy most certainly was losing her mind. Everything that happened had to be something that had come about in her own mind. Maybe she, Peggy, had been the one who had ripped the beloved teddy bear. Maybe it was she, Peggy, who scared her, Ginger, so badly that the cat wanted nothing more to do with being in the house, regardless of the comfort the home provided.

Peggy hadn't looked in the cedar chest but she feared what evil she may have done in there. Now, while she was having a reasonably sane moment, she must get help. Maybe call her granddaughter? Ask her to come out and take her to the doctor. There could be no other reason for all that was going on here. It must be just her creating all this madness.

Peggy got up from her chair and started to walk towards the house phone. As she passed the open stairway to the basement she felt a push to her side, sending her careening down the basement steps. She felt a push. Yes, she was sure it was a push.

"Well, was she sure?" Now lying at the bottom of the stairs, unable to move, the pain was so great, she couldn't remember. "Had she let herself fall? Had she planned all along to fall?" She couldn't remember. She didn't think she had gotten to the phone but couldn't remember that either. Peggy lay there, unable to move without fierce pain. No one to help. No way to help herself.

CHAPTER

NINE

Kathy had been instant messaging Peggy for a few days, but receiving no reply. This was Kathy's way of checking on her mother. If there wasn't a reply soon, Kathy would send her daughter out to check on her mother. With no reply on the second day, Kathy messaged her daughter, Hannah.

"Hannah, will you please go out and check on your grandmother? I'm sure she is alright, but just in case. And take Michael with you." Kathy messaged.

Hannah's current boyfriend Michael and Hannah drove out to the house. Nothing appeared to be amiss when they pulled up, but Michael had a bad feeling and asked Hannah to stay in the car while he checked things out. Hannah gave him the key that she carried and Michael walked into the house. Nothing seemed out of place, or indicated anything amiss. A torn up teddy bear on the sofa, a doll in the corner, but nothing out of the usual.

Michael called out for Peggy, but received no answer. He went upstairs, but he knew she rarely went upstairs. He looked through the main floor rooms … no Peggy. He started down to the basement, and at the bottom of the basement stairs he found her lying in a heap. Michael didn't make it all the way down. He saw her body at the bottom of the stairs. She didn't appear to be breathing even from where he was standing.

"How sad to end life with just a fall." Michael thought to himself. He called 911 before going back outside. He would let the authorities take care of the rest. Right now, he needed to be there for Hannah.

DEE'S
STORY

FOUR

That was not exactly how Dee had planned the story to go, but to be honest, she was just sick of this storyline.

"Might as well put this story in an early grave as well." She thought. "A dead end. What a play on words."

Dee closed down her computer and walked away from doll story. It had started out pretty good Dee thought, but she just couldn't go anywhere with it. No inspiring storyline at this time.

"And besides," Dee said to herself, "I am sick to death with thinking about that darn doll. Wish I could get my mind off death as well."

Dee began tidying up around the house. She did a few dishes and fixed herself some lunch. She sat down in her favorite chair and turned on the TV.

"Time to relax for a while." She thought. "When writing gets to be too straining on your mind, it is no longer a hobby." She was going to take some time off and just be lazy a while. Maybe take a nice long nap. That seemed to be her favorite past time anymore.

Dee was awake, but quite relaxed when she heard it again. The "click, click, click". Now she had taken the bride doll to the thrift store. She knew this sound couldn't have anything to do with the doll, but the first thing that came to mind was those little wooden feet stepping across her stone floors. It made the same sound as when she had "walked" the doll in her childhood.

"That damn doll is gone! Why am I still thinking about her?" Dee was getting upset with her obsessions with this doll. "I am going to find out where this clicking is coming from."

FIVE

Dee looked all about the house for what might be making that sound. It never lasted long, maybe 5 or six "clicks" at a time. Every time she heard it and gave the sound her attention, it stopped. So that made it hard to track down where it was coming from. But today she was tired and aggravated with herself and wanted to pin it down. Dee searched most of the day, but couldn't locate what might be compromised and making that clicking sound. She finally gave up and ended up back in her chair watching TV.

Days went by. The six or so "clicks" would awaken Dee in her sleep. She was tuned in now, almost waiting for the sound. She would hear them while working or resting in the house. She would attempt to track down where the sound was originating from, and never find it. She never find anything amiss. It was all beginning to work on her mind. And every time, without fail, in the back of her mind, it was connected to the doll. Somehow Dee knew, when she found the sound, she would find the doll. Waiting, ready to pounce on her in some way, ready to punish her for not taking care of her (the doll) and treating her as the royalty that the doll believed she was due. Dee knew this was ridiculous. She knew it couldn't possibly be that way. But the very thought of her bride doll kept creeping into her mind each time she had to deal with the clicking sound. The sound that told her the doll was "walking" toward her.

Dee had gotten to the point where she was not able to get any sleep or rest. She knew her health was suffering. She finally went to her doctor and discussed her health problems with her doctor. Of course, she did not share the ridiculous things she had been relating her troubles too. She was still sane enough to know how crazy that all sounded. And she did want to be taken seriously.

SIX

Her doctor suggested an in hospital stay just to get checked out. Dee thought this was a great idea and thought maybe she might get some good sleep in a new setting. She was looking forward to a good rest.

Dee checked herself in, with her doctor's orders, and settled back. Her nurse on duty at the time, came in to talk with her.

"Hi, I am Stephanie." The nurse said. "But you can call me Stephie. Please use your call light for anything you might need. We want you to get as much rest as possible. I believe they are going to do a sleep study soon. Can I get you anything right now?"

Dee assured her that she was fine. Stephie seemed like a nice person. It was good to have someone to talk to and someone to look after you. It was going to be a good night, and Dee settled back into her bed.

It wasn't long before she was sound asleep. Resting just like she knew she would once here. When she woke, she could tell it must be quite late. It was pretty dark outside her window. It was pretty quiet in the hall.

And then she heard it. "Click, click, click."

Only this time, it didn't stop with only a few clicks. This time it continued out in the hall. Getting louder with each step. And, yes, she knew now it was steps. She knew it was not in her mind anymore. This was the doll, walking by herself. Wooden feet on hard floors. She knew the sound. She had walked the doll many times in her childhood to the same sound of the little wooden feet on hard floors. The doll was coming for her.

Wrapped in her hospital blankets, too afraid to move, Dee counted the clicks as they grew louder and watched the door to her room slowly open.

CHAPTER

SEVEN

Nurse Stephanie talked with the doctor later that evening.

"She had come into the room," She said, "To check on her new patient and found her lying with bed sheets pulled up almost covering her face. A look of terror on her face. Eyes wide. Mouth slightly open, as though she were screaming."

"I don't know what happened, Doctor. She seemed fine just a few hours before. She had her call light right there, but there had been no attempts to call as far as we could see. Do you think it was a heart attack?"

EIGHT

We don't know what the power of the mind can do. Has it ever been fully tapped? Or is there truth to James Whitcomb Riley's poem, "An' the Gobble-uns'll git you Ef you don't watch out?"

CARRIE'S
LAST
DANCE

CHAPTER

ONE

"Carrie, it is almost your birthday," Nick said. "If you could have anything you wanted, go anywhere you wanted, what would you like for your birthday? Not saying I could afford it, but what would make your birthday special? After all, 83 is kind of important."

Carrie thought about this a while. "I don't know, what I like to do the best is nap. Ha! But I guess, if I could do anything, it would be nice to be able to go to another Johnny Cash concert, and dance in the front. That would be a little bit far-fetched because he has been dead a few years. About as likely that I could dance to even one song." Carrie replied.

Nick had been coming in to take care of Carrie for a couple years now. The arrangement had been set up by her family. They were a loving family but everyone lived out of state and they didn't get to visit quite as often as they would have liked. But so far, Carrie was doing okay on her own. She just needed a little help now and then, and that is where Nick came in. He took her to purchase groceries once a month. He kept the lawn mowed in the summer and the driveway cleared of snow in the winter. Carrie didn't go very far in the winter. She hadn't fired up the old Ford for a while now, but the area by the mailbox had to be kept clear of snow or the mail person wouldn't deliver the mail. Nick also stopped in just to chat, too. He was that kind of guy.

"Yup, that would be fun, wouldn't it?" Carrie went on, "I can think of a lot of entertainers that used to be, that I would like to listen to again. I wish I could even catch them on tv once in a while."

"Carrie, do you have internet access out here?" Nick asked.

Yes, that she did. The last time her son was home he set up the tv channels with something that needed internet. She knew she had internet but didn't use it much because she could never remember how to navigate. She watched her favorite shows on her little tv that used only a small antenna. Granted, she didn't get many channels that way, but it was way easier to figure out than the big tv with the many, many channels that you had to navigate through.

Nick, being young and knowledgeable about these things, attempted, like her children and grandchildren did when they visited, to teach her how to access what she might enjoy. And she did enjoy watching those shows, but that person would have to stay right there and set it up each and every time. Her memory wasn't what it used to be and all this wonderful knowledge would disappear as soon as that young person walked out the door. Carrie often wondered if it took that long for her children to figure out how to use a spoon. Probably not. We weren't so overloaded with information back in those days. But here Nick was again, navigating that big tv with its Roku or Firetv, or whatever it was set up to, and showing Carrie all the ways she could find Johnny Cash.

He finally settled on Youtube and where the little magnifying glass thingy was he put in Johnny Cash's name, and up popped all these songs Johnny Cash sang. Nick clicked on one and Carrie had the fine opportunity to listen and see him in concert again. Delightful!

Nick asked if there were anyone else she wanted to listen to, and Carrie chose Frank Sinatra. Again, Nick typed in Frank Sinatra where the little magnifying glass was and up popped a whole list of songs Frank sang. He really did have a lot of hits.

It was getting a little late in the day and Nick had to head out soon, so he showed Carrie again how she could get to this site. (Carrie planned to just leave it on this same spot and have it there for the next time. She wouldn't be accessing the big tv anyway for anything else). And Nick even wrote down on a paper how to put in the name, where to put it in, and left the paper on the stand next to Carrie's chair.

Carrie spent the rest of that evening listening to various artists. It had been a long time since she had enjoyed an evening so nice. As a matter of fact, most of Carrie's favorite musicians and actors had passed. That is kind of the way it is after you reach a certain age. Going back, even with this media, awakened her soul a little bit. She remembered the fun they used to have when they were younger. She remembered going to dances on Saturday nights in little towns that only may have had one workable street, but on Saturday nights those that worked a plow during the day, would bring their instruments and play till sometimes 2:00 in the morning. She remembered listening to shows like "The Statler Brothers", "Andy Williams Special", "The Ed Sullivan Show", "Hee Haw". So many great entertainers. All gone now. And the loved ones she enjoyed watching these shows with … gone as well. But listening again on this Youtube thing brought back a lot of that joy.

CHAPTER
TWO

Carrie lived alone and continued to take care of herself, with occasional help from Nick. There were little problems creeping up now and then, but for most she could count on Nick to help. She hated to ask him to come out too often though, so Carrie made sure she lived a simple life. Her medications came through the mail. Most of her bill paying was done through automatic pay through her bank (as was her social security deposit).

She was able to do the necessary things though, like shower, fix her meals, though she rarely cooked on the stove anymore, there had been an incident. Now she mainly relied on the microwave or, more often, made a sandwich. After all, it was just her. No need for a big meal. She could take care of her own laundry needs. She had plenty of clothes and no one to dress up for. Yes, she was doing rather well on her own.

Carrie usually spent her days feeding her birds and the feral cats. (She did what she could and what she could reach as far as the bird feeders were concerned. Years ago she had given up trying to keep her footing on any kind of step stool or ladder. Now she had enough trouble not tripping over her own feet with simply walking.)

Her life was quiet but it worked for her. She watched game shows and a couple soaps on her little tv. Fortunately, probably because she used it so much, she could always figure out how to tap into her favorite old shows (I Love Lucy, Gunsmoke, etc.). She watched too many crime shows and was a faithful attendee of House Hunters and International House Hunters, when she could navigate the big tv. Carrie, who had grown up with an outhouse, marveled at those who thought one or two bathrooms were not enough or were not fancy enough.

"That is not the decor I would have chosen." A frequent comment.

"You should have to walk through snow in the middle of the night to do your job," She thought

However, little things, like remembering to take the garbage out on the scheduled pick up days, getting the daily mail in, taking her daily pills. Little things seemed to get missed now and then. Carrie was not too concerned but she did notice things slipped her mind more often.
"Getting old, I guess." A comment that passed through her thoughts more and more.

It hadn't been too long ago that she had put the kettle on for tea and turned on the wrong burner, unknowingly. While she waited for the kettle to whistle, she napped a little bit, and woke to the fire alarm going off. The burner she had turned on was too close to the bread lying next to it on the counter, and had set the bread wrapper on fire. The alarm went off just as the fire touched on the cupboards above. Carrie jumped up and tried to put the fire out with the hand towel on the counter, but that also had caught fire, and Carrie burned herself just a little getting the burning hand towel to the sink. It wouldn't have been so bad but the fire had turned the under cupboards black before she could put it out.

Carrie knew she would need to "cover up" this incident. It would not look good to Nick or her family. She doctored her burnt hand herself. It hurt but she feared going in to the doctor. Too many questions would come up. She cleaned up the under cupboard that had been burned but it still showed blackened wood. She was afraid this would be her undoing when Nick saw it.

It gets that way as you get older, the need to "cover up" those little mishaps. And there gets to be more and more mishaps. The consequences of not being able to properly take care of yourself makes a person fearful. No telling when they were going to decide it was time to pack her up and place her in special care. There was no need to rush into these things. She loved her freedom, even if it was becoming increasingly limited.

"I'll do better, I'll be more careful," a continuing reminder to herself.

But Nick had started noticing that Carrie needed a little more help. He mentioned this to Carrie's daughter, Lynn. Lynn messaged Robert, Carrie's son, and they all group chatted about what was to be done next. Especially with winter coming on, mom was going to need more help. They had to consider her needs and what they could do. However, even Nick did not realize just how difficult things had gotten at Carrie's home.

—98—

CHAPTER
THREE

It was a brisk day in late October. A little chilly maybe for Wisconsin, but Wisconsin is funny that time of year. Sometimes it can be as warm as summer, sometimes you can get the worst winter storms in October. Trick or treating night can be miserable, with November being summerlike again. You just never knew what to expect in October, in Wisconsin.

Robert had rented a car at the airport and was driving back to his mother's home. Thankfully no snow, as Robert had lived in California for so long he had almost forgotten how to drive in snow. Carrie used to go pick him up but she had stopped driving for all means and purposes a while ago. He knew she would pick him up if he really needed her to, but he didn't think it was in the best interest of Carrie's, or any other driver on the highway, to ask her to do this.

Robert had told his mother he was coming home that week, but he also knew she would not remember. And she didn't. When he arrived at the house the furnace had not been turned on and it was cold in the house. He found Carrie burrowed under a big blanket. Her house cat trying to stay warm under the same blanket.

"Mom, why didn't you turn on the furnace?" Robert asked, a little irritated.

"It wasn't necessary yet." Carrie answered. But she also knew the truth was she couldn't figure out how to get the heat on. She knew the general area where the switch was located, but couldn't recall the sequence. She was not about to let her family know she needed someone to come out and turn on the heat for her. But, here she was, caught and cold.

"Well, let's get this place warmed up." He said and proceeded to set things in order.

Robert hadn't stopped to get groceries on the way home, and now it was snowing. He did not want to go out again, after a long flight and drive home. He looked through the refrigerator, finding really nothing but spoiled milk, which he quickly dumped. He then searched the freezer. At least in the freezer he found a roast. It had some freezer burn from being in there so long, but he checked it and decided he was hungry enough to cook it up.

Not much in the cupboards either. There was tuna in the cupboards but no bread. There was no mayo for making a sandwich with the tuna, and that was pretty much all he found in the cupboard. Even the cat food was gone. He didn't know what the poor cat had been eating. Looked like he was going to be driving to the little market down the road after all.

Carrie felt a little embarrassed that her son had found her in this predicament. Nick had been calling and checking on her, but Carrie refused to let on that she needed anything. Now she wished she would have asked Nick to help more. Carrie couldn't remember her son telling her he was coming home. If she had remembered, she would have been much more prepared. Dang it!

That night she heard her son upstairs talking to his wife. He usually talked to his wife on the loud speaker, but not tonight. Guess he didn't want his mom to know what they were talking about. After he talked to his wife, he called Lynn. And they talked quietly together as well.

Carrie could almost see the writing on the wall. Things were about to change.

CHAPTER

FOUR

Robert stayed for a little longer than he planned. He set up the house for Carrie for winter. Putting away summer outdoor chairs and equipment, setting up a few more agencies to come in and take care of winter needs. He also made arrangements with Nick to come out the same day as he left to make sure Carrie was going to be okay.

Robert also noticed the blackened cupboards and pressed her for an explanation, which she finally provided, though only in bits and pieces. He figured out the basic story line though. And he felt the concern. That day he unhooked the gas stove. There would be no more using the stove, even for a cup of tea.

What Robert didn't know was that she had almost ruined the microwave too. She had accidently put the bowl of soup on 33 minutes, instead of 3 to warm up the soup. Darn fingers must have gotten happy. She didn't notice the popping and steam of the boiling soup in the microwave window. When she did open the door to the microwave, soup had boiled over and splashed on the microwave walls, making a nasty mess to clean up.

Carrie was not about to tell him that story. She had not used the microwave for a while after that either. It was still working, thank goodness.

Evidently Lynn and Robert had talked quite a bit about what to do with mother, because the week after Robert left, and just a few days after Nick stopped in, Lynn and husband showed up at her door.

"Shoot! Did Lynn tell me that they were coming?" Carrie thought to herself. So many things Carrie couldn't remember anymore. Yes, she was concerned herself, but the other options just did not appeal to her. She loved her home and freedom. "Besides, what would become of her old friend, her cat?"

There had been a warm up in the weather between the last time Robert had been at the house and before Lynn and her husband had showed up. Now, once again, it was cold, and, once again, Carrie couldn't remember how to get the furnace going. She had managed to turn it off when it warmed up outside, but couldn't remember how to turn it back up again. There were always good days and bad days.

"Such a simple thing to work that furnace switch. Why could she not remember?" She thought to herself. It was so very frustrating to Carrie.

And, again, it was very cold in the house. Lynn's husband, Wyatt, began taking care of things much the same as her son had taken things in hand a few weeks earlier. Now it was down in November and it didn't seem like there was going to be another warming trend. Carrie needed that furnace going. This time she would make sure she left it where Wyatt put it.

Soon the house was warm again and Lynn and Wyatt settled in. The refrigerator had a little more available this time because before he left Robert had filled it up. Even the milk was still good. Cupboards were full, but it didn't look like anything had been used for meals. As a matter of fact, apart from some toast and a few cans of soup, Carrie had not made much for meals since Robert had left. Even the cat was tickled to see Lynn. The cat dish was empty again.

Lynn, Robert, and Nick all knew now that something would need to be done. Tomorrow would be soon enough to have the talk with Mom. Carrie could feel the weight of the necessary coming upon her. That night, thinking, sleep eluded her. She could see the nursing home coming, and Carrie knew it was probably something that was for her own good, but everything in her struggled against it. Sleep, even with the soothing music did not come easily that night. She did sleep fitfully and in spurts but always waking to that feeling of loss.

CHAPTER

FIVE

The next morning they had "The Talk". Lynn did her best to be gentle and tell her mother how important it was to have someone there to take care of her. Carrie, who had known this was coming for some time, chose to be as brave as she could be, not give any of her family any problems. After all, we all know this day is coming if we do not leave this world sooner than expected. It is never, ever when we had planned though. That personal freedom, doing things our way, living our own life, is so precious, it is so hard to give up. Carrie, filled with dread and sadness, helped Lynn sort through her things that she wanted to have with her, and they drove into town to the nursing facility that Lynn and Robert had already chosen. A long, quiet, sad drive.

It was a nice enough facility. It was warm, Carrie would give it that. A dang sauna in there, actually. The social worker met Lynn and Carrie at the door and ushered them to a room on the Memory Unit. A locked unit for those who would wander. Carrie noticed that one right away.

"Yeah, she would wander for sure. Right off the grounds if she got a chance." Carrie thought. "Good thing they keep that door locked."

The room was nice enough. A bed, dresser for your clothes. A small closet, and a night stand next to her bed with a little lamp. That would be nice for reading.

The lady in the bed next to hers had a wheelchair but it was on the other side of the room so it was not in Carrie's way. Carrie had some balance issues but her legs were still in working order so, even though her mind was failing, she could walk. The lady in the next bed said "Hello". The social worker introduced Betty (Carrie's roommate) to everyone. Betty

— 103 —

seemed very sweet, a little forgetful, but Betty's mind seemed to be in better shape than her body.

Carrie was introduced to all those working in the hall that day. Lunch was about to be served and the CNA came and took Carrie to lunch. Lynn was also invited and she stayed to have lunch with Carrie. After lunch Lynn gave her mother a hug and asked her to just give it a try for a few days. Carrie said she would do that and put on a brave smile. She knew there would not be "just a few days". This would be her home now. There had been plenty of hardship in her life and this was just a new chapter. Time to dig in and stay strong. Time to give her children the chance to live their own lives without worrying about her. Carrie kept telling herself these things, trying to stay strong, but it was not working in the very heart of her. She was terrified, and oh, so very sad. Getting old is not for the weak.

CHAPTER

SIX

"Aaaagh! Help! You're trying to drown me!" The CNA was trying to give Carrie a shower. The hand held shower tap was coming down on her head and her face, and no one had warned Carrie that this was about to happen. It was warm enough, just a surprise.

"Waterboarding! That's what it is. You are trying to kill me!" She thought as her arms flayed and she tried to dodge the hand held shower. "How in the hell can I remember 'waterboarding' and I can't remember how to turn on the damn heat?" She thought. "The mind sure is a mysterious thing."

With all her screaming and thrashing of arms, the CNA had stopped and was trying to calm her, but Carrie was in no mood to be calmed.

"And you don't wash my face <u>after</u> you have washed my arm pits." Carrie yelled at the young girl. "That is not how I shower."

Everyone has their own way of doing things. From simple tasks such as brushing your teeth to taking a shower. We all have our own process. Those who no longer are able to do these things themselves still remember the "proper" way to do such tasks … their way.

The poor CNA finally managed to get the shower completed and Carrie into warm clothes. By this time though, Carrie was shivering ferociously. Now she was glad someone had brought the sweatshirt and sweat pants.

Next, the CNA helped Carrie get to breakfast. Meals in a nursing facilty are interesting. A nursing facility is carefully monitored by government agencies, and the staff keep close tabs on what each resident eats and whether they are losing or gaining weight.

Carrie usually had coffee and toast for breakfast. Today, on her plate she saw scrambled eggs. (An almost constant at a nursing home.) She also had a couple sausages (Carrie hated sausage links), toast, milk, juice, coffee, and oatmeal (always there is oatmeal).

"How in hell am I going to eat all of this," Carrie thought to herself. She ate the toast and had her coffee. Then she sat back to look at the others at the table. And then the "encouragement" started.

"Carrie, can you eat a little more of the eggs, please?" The nurse asked.

"I'm full." Carrie said.

"Try some of the juice then." The CNA encouraged.

And this went on and on throughout the meal. Staff encouraging, Carrie digging in her heels. If she had been starving she wouldn't have eaten another bite. Finally staff gave up and they began clearing the tables for activity participation.

Another staff person came in at this point and ushered Carrie into another room for some entertainment. This staff put on some nice music, music that was to Carrie's liking, and they began to sing along, with the words running just under the entertainer who was singing on the tv monitor. Much like Mitch Miller, for those who can remember Mitch Miller. Carrie did enjoy this time of her day. A melody of voices, mostly aging voices, were all singing along to old songs, whether you could read the words or not, it didn't matter, most of them could remember the words to these songs.

"Memory is like that. I can't recall my cat's name, but I can remember every word to this song", Carrie though. "And where is Cat?" She wondered.

The few hours went by quickly and Carrie didn't even want to go anywhere else. It was a pleasant time. Carrie didn't even miss her home too much. Then it was lunch time. Again! Already! And she stared at her plate of chicken, vegetable, small salad, and cookie. Milk, juice, water. She hadn't even moved any body parts but her voice. Where was she going to put more food? The same encouragement began again. Again, Carrie digging in, she resolved not to eat but a bite or two of chicken and a little milk. This war was getting old fast. Well, maybe she would have her cookie.

"I would like a Diet Coke, please," Carrie requested.

"We don't have Diet Coke, Carrie," the CNA explained.

"I always have a Diet Coke in the afternoon," Carrie said.

"I'm sorry, Carrie, we don't have Diet Coke here. Can you drink your juice?"

Now, anyone who enjoys their Diet Coke or Diet Pepsi knows you can't replace that with juice. It might have been a very small thing, but this very small thing was something Carrie enjoyed, and you can be brave and strong just so long. Carrie got up from the table and looked for a phone on the unit to call Lynn. There was not a phone to be found anywhere. These little struggles were getting more and more difficult to accept.

Carrie walked back to her room, and that is where the nurse found her crying on her bed.

"Carrie, what is wrong? What can I help you with?" The nurse asked.

Carrie explained that she needed to talk to her daughter or son. Maybe even Nick if the other two were not available. The nurse did call the number left by Lynn, and Lynn and Wyatt were still at the house. Lynn talked to Carrie through the nurse's phone.

"Mom, it is only a couple days. What is wrong?" Lynn asked.

Carrie tried to explain the struggles she was going through, but is was difficult for Lynn to relate. Finally Carrie asked if Lynn could bring her out some Diet Coke and maybe some Twinkies, or any snack item.

Lynn and Wyatt had called Nick and he showed up that afternoon with Diet Coke and packages of Twinkies and bite size candies. (Much to the dismay of the unit nurse).

"We try to discourage this kind of a diet." The nurse explained. We try to keep a healthy diet for our residents.

Nick understood the nurse's concern, but everyone has one or two little sins. He asked if they could keep these here for her just for now and maybe over time Carrie would adjust to a healthier diet. (Probably not likely but it was worth a try). The nurse accepted this for now, but was hesitant.

Carrie didn't want any of these treats to leave her room, so she tucked them away in the drawer of her dresser. Warm Diet Coke was better than none.

CHAPTER
SEVEN

Days at the nursing home became weeks. Carrie had learned to adapt to the many, many rules, including locked doors, windows that would not raise, the minimum amount you could get by with eating at every meal, no touring around the halls after bed time, and on and on and on.

"Might as well be a prison." Carrie thought.

She did enjoy special entertainers that came in once in a while though. It was coming up on Christmas now and there seemed to be a lot of new people coming and going on her unit. People who enjoyed singing, enjoyed visiting with each resident. She enjoyed doing crafts and some movies. She did not enjoy shower days or middle of the night vital checks. She would finally fall asleep and there would be someone by her bed checking on her. Darn near gave her a heart attack sometimes.

Carrie hadn't seen her family in some time, but they were busy with work and their lives. She didn't expect to see them often. Nick, even though he was no longer on the payroll, stopped in, and when he stopped, he brought those little treats she loved so much. Snuck them in now, and hid them in the same dresser drawer. These things had a way of disappearing quickly though. Certain staff knew there would be a sweet snack in there and often helped themselves to Carrie's snack drawer, even the soda.

A little after the new year, Lynn and Wyatt came to visit. They brought Christmas gifts and stayed the entire day. It was cold outside so they chose not to take her out, but Carrie totally enjoyed the day with them. She could remember both their names, and Carrie was thrilled with being able to remember them so completely that day. Her memory was continuing to slip away from her. They brought pictures of her cat. A grandchild was taking care of her cat now and had named him "Buster". Buster looked well. But Carrie couldn't remember much about "Cat" that day. He looked like a nice cat though and Carrie was glad he was cared for.

About a month later, Robert got away from his job and came to visit. They spent the day together and what a pleasant day that had been.

Over Christmas Nick had stopped by. He brought a gift for Christmas as well. A tablet. He set it all up for Carrie. He explained that all you had to do was … "Blah, Blah, Blah!" You might as well have been teaching rocket science. For Carrie it went in one ear and out the other. But Nick left the tablet on the night stand next to Carrie's bed.

Carrie was having more and more trouble sleeping at night. She often would get out of bed and roam about her room. She had quickly learned she could not roam about the halls, but if she stayed quiet, she could move about the room without attracting attention from the staff. She did tend to keep her roommate awake though, and she was sorry for that, but she just could not stay in bed.

One night, as the CNA on duty, Linda, passed Carrie's room, she heard this quiet little voice singing. "Moon River, wider than a mile, I'm crossing you in style someday…" Carrie couldn't remember all the words, so many times she would just fill in with humming.

Linda stood outside the room for a while, just listening. Finally she quietly pushed open the door a little bit. Linda found Carrie over by the window, looking out into the darkness and still singing/humming.

"Carrie, would you like to list'en to that song on your tablet?" Linda asked. The tablet had been sitting, untouched, on the bedside stand since Nick had left it.

Carrie was startled that someone had come into the room, and even more startled that they had heard her singing, but the option of listening to the music was interesting to her and she agreed to this right away.

"We can put the music on low enough that it won't bother Betty. Maybe she will even enjoy it also." Linda said.

And with that, Linda started setting up the tablet so Carrie could listen to music. Linda put the volume low enough that Carrie could hear it and sing along if she chose, but at a volume that would not be disturbing to the other resident. Carrie sat down, eventually lying down, next to the tablet and sang along with every song that came up until she finally fell asleep. Linda came in a short time later and covered her up and turned off the tablet. And with this, the evening ritual of singing, falling asleep with Frank Sinatra, Dean Martin, Steve Lawrence, Johnny Cash, Elvis Presley, and so many more, began. Every time Linda worked she would set up the tablet for Carrie, put it on various artist, and then come back in and cover Carrie and turn off the tablet. This worked so well with getting Carrie to settle down for the night, Linda quickly trained other CNAs and staff to do the same.

CHAPTER

EIGHT

arrie had learned how to comply with expectations at the nursing facililty. It just became easier that way. Staff had begun feeding her. Not because she could no longer feed herself, she just didn't choose to eat everything on her plate. And often, even with help from staff, she would not open her mouth for another bite. She just couldn't manage another bite. Staff continued to try but knew it would be useless once Carrie would not open her mouth, and they learned to get through meals gracefully, eventually.

After the evening meal, there was always an activity in the social room of the unit. Sometimes it was a pleasant activity, sometimes Carrie just sat back in her chair and thought about her past, her family, or her life before the nursing home, when she could recall these things. Staff learned if she didn't want to talk, if she didn't want to participate, they would allow her time to reflect on whatever her mind wanted to dwell on. Cooperation on both ends made life a little more pleasant.

Around 7:00 in the evening, and sometimes a little before, staff would begin taking individuals back to their rooms to get them ready for the night's rest. Carrie, still able to ambulate, soon became one of the last to go to her room and get ready for bed. Carrie's roommate, now another lady, would already be in bed and sometimes appeared to be sleeping, though Carrie often thought she would only appear to be sleeping. A couple of times Carrie would notice her new roommate watching her.

Staff helped Carrie get into her night clothes. They help her into bed and turned off the light, with the exception of the bathroom light in case Carrie needed to get up in the night. The resident's all had call lights to ask for assistance, but whether stubborn (often the case on Carrie's part) or forgetfulness, the call lights were seldom employed. Then, leaving the door slightly ajar, the staff would leave for the night. They would occasionally peek in to make sure everything was okay, but generally they allowed for the residents to have peaceful sleep. The only time they came in would be for vital checks or medicine pass.

The perception of how things went at bedtime was a little different in Carrie's reality. She thought maybe it might be a little far-fetched but she had been enjoying these evening activities and thought better than to question what was happening. After the staff left the room, and before the tablet came as a gift, Carrie would remember an old song and start singing to herself … singing quietly as not to awaken her roommate. She could not always recall all the words so she would hum through the "wordless" parts and then pick up when the words come back into her memory.

One night, as she got out of bed and walked over to the window, she was singing into the darkness of the night and a face appeared in the window, like a tv screen. She had been singing "Try To Remember", and who should appear in the window, but Andy Williams. Carrie had been humming mostly because she could barely remember past, "Try to remember", but then Andy picked up the song, and sang it through. It was delightful. Andy Williams had such a lovely voice. And this song had such a beautiful thought to it. Try to remember, hadn't she been doing this a long time now? And Andy singing to her through the window "tv", just brought her to that peaceful moment. The moments she needed before lying down for the night.

So every night now, Carrie would go to the window after she thought staff had gone and her roommate had fallen asleep, and try to think of a song she wanted to sing to herself. And, like magic, whatever song she wanted to sing would be followed by that artist coming to her window "tv" screen and singing with her. With the help of the artist she could almost remember all the words too, though it didn't really matter, she enjoyed their singing more than her own.

After the tablet came for Christmas she no longer got out of bed. Being able to listen to the various artist that Linda or the other staff would set up for her would be enough. It was almost like they were there. But then one night, as she lay with her head on her pillow, listening to Bobby Darin sing

"Mack the Knife", and there he was, sitting on the edge of her bed, singing right along with the tablet. Yeah, Carrie was not going to tell anyone about this. Highly unlikely, she knew this, but she sure enjoyed it. Who would not want Bobby Darin sitting on the edge of their bed. And every night after that, someone would come to her bed, usually someone from the play list, and sing to her. It was the very best way to fall asleep.

CHAPTER
NINE

Months passed. The children were still both in different states. Nick didn't come as often but once in a while he stopped in. Carrie had adjusted to life in the facility. Her physical health had begun to fail, slowly at first, but now there seemed to be more problems every day. She was still able to walk, but tripped often and staff had been looking into getting her a wheelchair. She did not want a wheelchair but had learned long ago that what she wanted didn't carry much weight around here. Carrie had overheard that her heart might not be working quite as well, but then, every bit of her was getting older. You can't expect parts to last forever.

Carrie still listened to her music before sleep. Her visitors didn't come so often. Maybe they came and she had already fallen asleep. That was possible because she was exhausted all the time anymore. She fell asleep pretty fast, often before this new roommate, (another new roommate) fell asleep. This roommate was young compared to Carrie, younger than many of the other residents here. Carrie didn't even know why she was at this facility. She seemed like she would do quite well on her own.

Tonight, just as she was about to fall asleep, a good old song came on the play list. One a new CNA had set up for her. "Rock Around the Block." Oh my, how many years ago had that been?

Carrie started singing along. "One, Two, Three O'Clock, Four O'Clock Rock, Five, Six, Seven O'Clock, Eight O'Clock Rock. Nine, Ten, Eleven O'Clock, Twelve O'Clock Rock. We're Going To Rock Around The Clock Tonight."

That was all she knew and began humming. And just like that she felt someone sit on the edge of her bed. Carrie opened her eyes and there sat a young man.

He introduced himself and his friends in the corner of the room. He said his name was Bill Haley and the guys in the corner are called The Comets. And they sang the entire song for her. Quietly, of course, if you can sing that song quietly. But it didn't appear to upset anyone, not even her roommate, who was watching Carrie closely from her own bed.

After they finished singing, Bill Haley asked Carrie if she wanted to dance with him. It had been so very long since Carrie had danced even a little bit, but she was not about to pass this up.

"Yes, yes," she said happily. "I don't know how long I can do it, but I sure want to dance."

And Carrie got up, took Bill's hand and they turned and swirled and then Bill would pull her in and they danced up close. It was heavenly. Everything her mind could recall of how things used to be. How delightful those things, we took for granted at the time, really were. She had a smile on her face as big as the moon. She threw her head back and laughed out loud.

Just a few twirls and Carrie was exhausted. She told Bill she had to lie down on her bed and rest just a bit, but she wanted to dance some more as soon as she got her wind back.

CHAPTER

TEN

Carrie's roommate finally found the call light button. She had been searching for it since Carrie had first gotten out of bed. The roommate was concerned Carrie was going to fall the way she was moving about. The staff finally came into the room and found Carrie lying across her bed, like she had fallen backward on it.

"She just started jumping around and flaying her arms like something was wrong, and I couldn't get her to listen to me. She was singing, of course. What is wrong with her?" The roommate was a little upset at this point and was worried about Carrie.

"You go back to sleep if you can, Sandra," The CNA said. We will take care of her.

They drew the curtain that separates one bed from the other, but the roommate, Sandra, was able to tell they were also concerned and attempting to take vitals and awaken Carrie. But there would be no awakening this time, not to this world. Carrie had danced her way to the next life with Bill Haley and His Comets. A big smile, rapidly waning, on her face.

"Life is a Hoot!

ELEVEN

have heard, if you walk by room number 34 at Northwoods Nursing Home, sometimes you can hear a scratchy, but happy voice singing "Moon River".

www.ingramcontent.com/pod-product-compliance
Lightning Source LLC
Chambersburg PA
CBHW070842160726
48004CB00001B/468